Diseases and Disorders

Ovarian Cancer

Titles in the Diseases and Disorders series include:

Acne
AIDS
Alzheimer's Disease
Anorexia and Bulimia
Anthrax
Arthritis
Asthma
Attention Deficit Disorder
Autism
Bipolar Disorder
Breast Cancer
Cerebral Palsy
Chronic Fatigue Syndrome
Cystic Fibrosis
Diabetes
Down Syndrome
Dyslexia
Epilepsy
Fetal Alchohol Syndrome
Headaches
Heart Disease
Hemophilia
Hepatitis
Learning Disabilities
Leukemia
Lyme Disease
Multiple Sclerosis
Obesity
Parkinson's Disease
Phobias
SARS
Schizophrenia
Sexually Transmitted Diseases
Sleep Disorders
Smallpox
Teen Depression
West Nile Virus

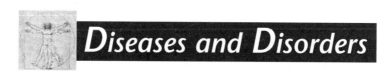
Diseases and Disorders

Ovarian Cancer

by Barbara Sheen

LUCENT BOOKS

An imprint of Thomson Gale, a part of The Thomson Corporation

THOMSON
™
GALE

Detroit • New York • San Francisco • San Diego • New Haven, Conn.
Waterville, Maine • London • Munich

GALE

On cover: A cancer patient undergoes chemotherapy treatment.

LIBRARY OF CONGRESS CATALOGING-IN-PUBLICATION DATA

Sheen, Barbara.
   Ovarian cancer / by Barbara Sheen.
   p. cm. — (Diseases and disorders)
Includes bibliographical references and index.
Contents: What is ovarian cancer?—Confusing symptoms and a difficult diagnosis—Conventional and complementary treatment—Living with ovarian cancer—What the future holds.
   ISBN 1-59018-342-8 (hardcover : alk. paper)
   1. Ovaries—Cancer—Juvenile literature. I. Title. II. Series: Diseases and disorders series.
   RC280.O8.S546 2003
   616.99'465—dc22
                                                                                    2004019013

Printed in the United States of America

Table of Contents

Foreword   6

Introduction
    When Knowledge Saves Lives   8

Chapter 1
    What Is Ovarian Cancer?   13

Chapter 2
    Confusing Symptoms and a Difficult Diagnosis   30

Chapter 3
    Conventional and Complementary Treatment   46

Chapter 4
    Living with Ovarian Cancer   62

Chapter 5
    What the Future Holds   78

    Notes   93
    Glossary   97
    Organizations to Contact   99
    For Further Reading   101
    Works Consulted   103
    Index   106
    Picture Credits   111
    About the Author   112

"The Most Difficult Puzzles Ever Devised"

CHARLES BEST, one of the pioneers in the search for a cure for diabetes, once explained what it is about medical research that intrigued him so. "It's not just the gratification of knowing one is helping people," he confided, "although that probably is a more heroic and selfless motivation. Those feelings may enter in, but truly, what I find best is the feeling of going toe to toe with nature, of trying to solve the most difficult puzzles ever devised. The answers are there somewhere, those keys that will solve the puzzle and make the patient well. But how will those keys be found?"

Since the dawn of civilization, nothing has so puzzled people—and often frightened them, as well—as the onset of illness in a body or mind that had seemed healthy before. A seizure, the inability of a heart to pump, the sudden deterioration of muscle tone in a small child—being unable to reverse such conditions or even to understand why they occur was unspeakably frustrating to healers. Even before there were names for such conditions, even before they were understood at all, each was a reminder of how complex the human body was, and how vulnerable.

While our grappling with understanding diseases has been frustrating at times, it has also provided some of humankind's most heroic accomplishments. Alexander Fleming's accidental discovery in 1928 of a mold that could be turned into penicillin has resulted in the saving of untold millions of lives. The isolation of the enzyme insulin has reversed what was once a death sentence for anyone with diabetes. There have been great strides in combating conditions for which there is not yet a cure, too. Medicines can help AIDS patients live longer, diagnostic tools such as mammography and ultrasounds can help doctors find tumors while they are treatable, and laser surgery techniques have made the most intricate, minute operations routine.

This "toe-to-toe" competition with diseases and disorders is even more remarkable when seen in a historical continuum. An astonishing amount of progress has been made in a very short time. Just two hundred years ago, the existence of germs as a cause of some diseases was unknown. In fact, it was less than 150 years ago that a British surgeon named Joseph Lister had difficulty persuading his fellow doctors that washing their hands before delivering a baby might increase the chances of a healthy delivery (especially if they had just attended to a diseased patient)!

Each book in Lucent's Diseases and Disorders series explores a disease or disorder and the knowledge that has been accumulated (or discarded) by doctors through the years. Each book also examines the tools used for pinpointing a diagnosis, as well as the various means that are used to treat or cure a disease. Finally, new ideas are presented—techniques or medicines that may be on the horizon.

Frustration and disappointment are still part of medicine, for not every disease or condition can be cured or prevented. But the limitations of knowledge are being pushed outward constantly; the "most difficult puzzles ever devised" are finding challengers every day.

When Knowledge Saves Lives

A MY STARTED FEELING ill when she was eighteen. She had a variety of different symptoms, such as fatigue and a swollen abdomen. Over the next two years, she visited a number of doctors and was given a different diagnosis by each one. Amy was twenty before the real cause of her symptoms was discovered: She had ovarian cancer.

A Rare and Dangerous Disease

Thousands of other women have the same experience as Amy. They, too, feel vaguely ill with a number of symptoms, which neither they nor their doctors link to ovarian cancer. A 1999 survey of ovarian cancer survivors conducted by University of Washington gynecologic oncologist Barbara Goff proved this point. The survey found that 26 percent of the women surveyed were not diagnosed with ovarian cancer for at least six months after they first sought medical help. Eleven percent were not correctly diagnosed for more than a year. This may be due to the fact that, compared with other forms of cancer, ovarian cancer is relatively rare and thus not generally suspected by doctors. Breast cancer, for example, strikes about 200,000 American women annually. Approximately 79,000 cases of lung cancer and 75,000 cases of colon cancer are reported each year. Ovarian cancer, on the other hand, strikes approximately 25,000 American women each year.

Although ovarian cancer strikes fewer people than many other types of cancer, it is the fifth leading cause of cancer deaths

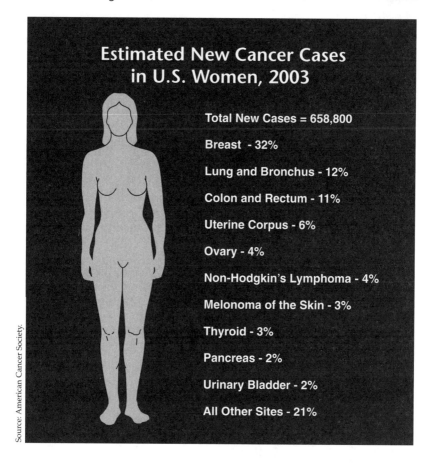

Estimated New Cancer Cases
in U.S. Women, 2003

Total New Cases = 658,800

Breast - 32%

Lung and Bronchus - 12%

Colon and Rectum - 11%

Uterine Corpus - 6%

Ovary - 4%

Non-Hodgkin's Lymphoma - 4%

Melonoma of the Skin - 3%

Thyroid - 3%

Pancreas - 2%

Urinary Bladder - 2%

All Other Sites - 21%

Source: American Cancer Society.

in American women, the deadliest of all cancers that affect the female reproductive system. It kills about fourteen thousand women in the United States each year.

Despite the threat it poses, ovarian cancer garners little attention from the media or the health care industry. Amy's mother explains, "I've been to so many doctors' offices when Amy was sick, and I've never seen any information on ovarian cancer."[1]

Lack of Awareness

Part of the problem is that ovarian cancer is difficult to recognize. Most diseases are characterized by recognizable symptoms that affect all individuals with the disease. Such is not the case in ovarian cancer, where the symptoms are often indistinct and vary from patient to patient. This is why ovarian cancer is frequently described as "the disease that whispers."

The lack of concrete symptoms of ovarian cancer makes it difficult to alert the public about what to look for, and keeps many women from seeking prompt medical care. Indeed, many women are unaware that the disease has any symptoms. Sheryl, whose sister died of ovarian cancer in 2000, explains: "I have met and heard the stories of many ovarian cancer survivors whose stories were nearly identical. Prior to being diagnosed, none had known that the symptoms they experienced were related to ovarian cancer. All were shocked by their diagnoses."[2]

Becoming Aware

When someone or something whispers, a microphone can be used to amplify the message. In the case of ovarian cancer, the "microphone" is the patients, and their friends and families, who are vocal about what they have learned. Awareness of the signs and symptoms of ovarian cancer can save lives. It can help indi-

Oncologists use ultrasound equipment to detect abnormalities in the reproductive organs of a woman who suspects she may have ovarian cancer.

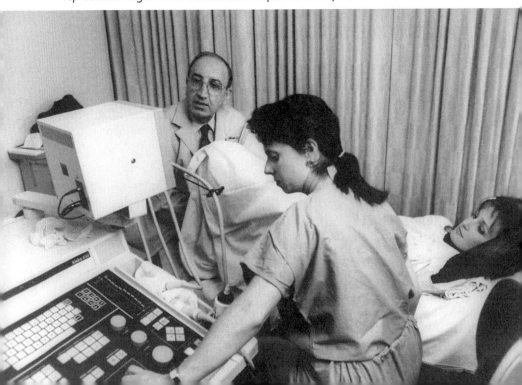

viduals to listen to their bodies more carefully, and seek early intervention when suspicious symptoms first appear. This can greatly increase a patient's chance of survival. About 90 percent of all patients with ovarian cancer survive for more than five years when the disease is detected and treated early. The statistics are more grim when the disease goes undetected and untreated. Five-year survival rates fall to as low as 20 percent once the disease has advanced. Amy's mother notes, "If I had read about the symptoms sooner, I might have recognized them much earlier."[3]

Learning the risk factors of ovarian cancer can help women who are at risk of the disease to be more vigilant. Although one out of every fifty-five women in the general population is likely to develop ovarian cancer, approximately one in twenty at-risk women contracts ovarian cancer each year. Yet many women are unaware of what factors put them at risk.

Bobbie Gostout is the communications chairperson of the Gynecologic Cancer Foundation, a group whose goal is to educate the public about ovarian and other cancers that affect the female reproductive system. She explains:

> The level of public education and awareness about gynecological cancers [ovarian, cervical, and uterine cancer] has been inadequate until now. Although public education efforts and media coverage regarding breast cancer screening has made women keenly aware of the importance of mammograms and self–breast examinations, the same cannot be said for gynecologic cancer. Far too many patients . . . say they did not know the warning signs or symptoms of various gynecologic cancers until they were diagnosed with one of these cancers. Many didn't learn—until they or a family member were diagnosed— that they possessed one or more known risk factors that elevated their risk above that of the general population.[4]

On the other hand, a woman who knows she is at risk for ovarian cancer can take steps to monitor her health and, thus, detect the disease early on. Similarly, knowing more about ovarian cancer can help women with the disease to cope better and live longer. It can help them select the best treatment available, as well as providing them with knowledge about what to expect as their treatment progresses. It can help their friends and families to deal with their own fears and anxieties, permitting them to provide their loved ones with the care and support they need. Such support can heighten a patient's chance of recovery.

In fact, learning about ovarian cancer is so important that in 2003, President George W. Bush declared September to be "Ovarian Cancer Awareness Month." In a proclamation to the nation, the president explained:

> We seek to increase the understanding of ovarian cancer. . . . I urge all women to talk to their doctors about ovarian cancer and the best course of action to detect and treat this deadly disease. . . . And I urge individuals across the country to learn more about this disease and what can be done to reduce the number of individuals who suffer from it. . . . Through education and continued research we can fight against ovarian cancer and save the lives of thousands of American women.[5]

Chapter 1

What Is Ovarian Cancer?

O VARIAN CANCER is a form of cancer that develops in the ovaries, a pair of small oval organs that are part of a woman's reproductive system. Since the ovaries are part of the female reproductive system and are not found in males, only women can get ovarian cancer.

Located inside a woman's pelvis, the ovaries produce the female hormone estrogen. The ovaries also release eggs at monthly intervals, which are either fertilized by a male's sperm or shed from the body when a woman menstruates.

Ovarian cancer develops when mutated cells in the ovaries grow uncontrollably and without a purpose. Besides causing problems in the ovaries, these cells can break away from the ovaries and spread to other parts of the body. These two characteristics, the uncontrollable growth of cells and the ability of those cells to spread throughout the body, define cancer.

Cells and Cancer

The human body is composed of cells, which, in a well-regulated process, grow, divide, and create more cells when the body needs them. When a cell gets old and can no longer do its job, it dies and a healthy new cell is manufactured to replace it.

Genes within each cell regulate this process, signaling to the cell when it is time to divide and when it is time to stop. Two genes in particular are essential for this process to work properly. The first, the oncogene, signals cells to divide. The second, the tumor suppressor gene, stops the process. Sometimes, due to cell

Female Reproductive System

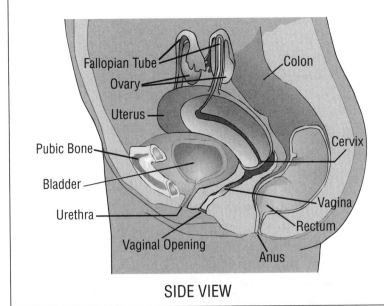

FRONT VIEW

Fallopian Tubes
Uterus
Ovary
Ovary
Uterine Soft Lining
Cervix
Vulva
Vagina

SIDE VIEW

Fallopian Tube
Ovary
Uterus
Pubic Bone
Bladder
Urethra
Vaginal Opening
Colon
Cervix
Vagina
Rectum
Anus

mutations, the oncogene becomes overstimulated, causing rapid cell growth, or the tumor suppressor gene ceases to function. As a result, even when new cells are not required, the mutated cells continuously divide without stopping. When ovarian cells are involved, the result is ovarian cancer.

In some women, the likelihood of this process occurring is inherited. In others, ovarian cancer cell mutation is random and spontaneous. In either case, as mutated cells divide, they bump together, and over time they form an abnormal mass or growth known as a malignant or cancerous tumor. Sometimes normal cells, too, bump together and form masses or tumors. However, unlike malignant tumors, these tumors are not composed of mutated cells, so their cells do not divide and increase without a purpose. Such tumors, known as benign tumors, are not cancerous.

Malignant tumors, on the other hand, keep increasing in size as more and more mutated cells form. As the tumor expands, it competes with and crowds out normal cells, seizing blood, oxygen, and nutrients, which all cells need to survive. Without sufficient blood, oxygen, and nutrients, healthy cells become unable to do their jobs effectively, and eventually they starve and die.

No Help from the Immune System

Since cancer cells are mutated from normal cells, the immune system does not recognize them as harmful. Normally, when a foreign substance threatens the body, the brain signals the immune system to send white blood cells and powerful chemicals called antibodies to attack and destroy the threat. However, cancer cells are not a foreign substance. They have the same chemical makeup as healthy cells. So, the immune system treats cancer cells as if they are normal cells, leaving them to grow without any response from the immune system.

Massachusetts Institute of Technology biology professor Robert A. Weinberg explains: "Tumors are not foreign invaders. They arise from the same material used by the body to construct its own tissues. Tumors use the same components—human cells—to form the jumbled masses that disrupt biological order

What Do the Ovaries Do?

In the book *100 Questions & Answers About Ovarian Cancer*, authors Don Dizon, Nadeem R. Abu-Rustum, and Andrea Gibbs Brown explain the function of the ovaries:

> The ovaries, fallopian tubes, and uterus are what make up a woman's internal female reproductive organs. These organs lie deep in the pelvis and are connected to one another. The cervix is the external extension of the uterus, and together with the vagina and vulva, forms the female external genital tract.

> Each woman is born with two ovaries, located on either side of the pelvis and flanking the uterus. Other organs are located near the ovaries: the small bowel and the omentum; the bladder, which sits on top of the uterus; and the rectum, which lies under the uterus.

> The ovaries are where eggs are stored. The ovaries start to release eggs when girls reach adolescence, and their bodies prepare for possible pregnancy by the release of hormones called estrogen and progesterone. Eggs are released at monthly intervals (called ovulation), and their release begins the menstrual cycle.

> The ovaries are essential as the home to these eggs until they're released into the fallopian tube and travel to the uterus. If an egg is not fertilized, the uterus sheds its lining. This process is manifest as menstruation, or your period. The ovaries not only carry a woman's eggs; they are also responsible for the release of estrogen that causes breast development and other sexual characteristics in women.

> As a woman ages, the ovaries slowly stop producing hormones, which results in menopause. During menopause, the process of egg release slows down and eventually stops.

and function and, if left unchecked, to bring the whole complex, life-sustaining edifice that is the human body crashing down."[6]

Tumors Spread

Left unchecked, the tumor often grows into surrounding organs, which in ovarian cancer are the fallopian tubes, uterus, bladder, colon, and peritoneum (the large membrane that insulates the abdomen). Cancer cells gain entry into these organs by producing an enzyme, or chemical, called protease, which breaks down connective tissues.

Making matters worse, cancer cells often break free from the tumor in a process known as shedding. Once free, the cells are carried through the bloodstream and/or the lymphatic system, which carries white blood cells throughout the body. In this

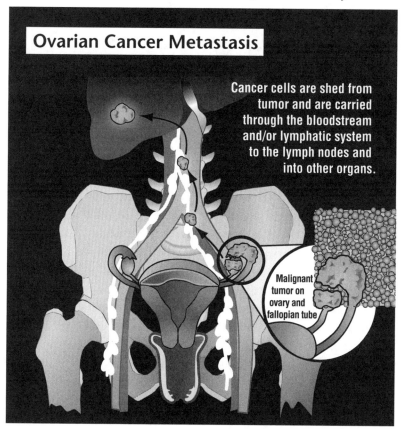

Ovarian Cancer Metastasis

Cancer cells are shed from tumor and are carried through the bloodstream and/or lymphatic system to the lymph nodes and into other organs.

Malignant tumor on ovary and fallopian tube

manner, cancer cells are transported to other organs, where they continue dividing, growing, and forming new tumors. The new tumors cause damage wherever they grow. This process is known as metastasis. Seventy percent of all cases of ovarian cancer metastasize.

Ovarian cancer cells can spread to any organ in the body and may affect a woman's liver, lungs, and brain. But due to their proximity, they most often infect the pelvis and abdominal cavity, and the organs therein. This part of the body, also known as the midsection, is bordered by the lungs and diaphragm on top and by the pubic bone on the bottom. Organs in a woman's midsection include the uterus, fallopian tubes, cervix, kidneys, colon, small and large intestines, bladder, stomach, peritoneum, and diaphragm. Comedian Gilda Radner, who lost her life to ovarian cancer, explained:

> I didn't just have ovarian cancer. It had spread to my bowel and my liver, but the cells hadn't eaten into those organs. They were just lying on top of those organs. . . . Ovarian cancer is extremely fast-growing. It's very insidious. All of a woman's major organs are down there in the same cavity, so even though the primary location of the cancer was the ovary, it was jumping around to other organs.[7]

Physical Effects of Ovarian Cancer

Whether or not ovarian cancer spreads beyond the ovaries, it has a physical effect on women with the disease. And if ovarian cancer is unchecked, its physical effects worsen as the cancer spreads. As an ovarian cancer tumor grows, it often presses on surrounding organs such as the colon, bladder, and abdomen, causing pain and making it difficult for these organs to function properly. If the tumor obstructs the colon, it becomes difficult for feces to pass through and be eliminated. Instead, feces back up, causing painful gas and constipation. In order to allow feces to pass by the tumor, the colon may swell. Sometimes, it becomes so enlarged that it tears. This can be life threatening.

Ovarian cancer often causes acute pain in the abdominal area. This patient in the terminal stage of the disease must lie on her side for relief.

The tumor can also obstruct the intestines, leading to indigestion and heartburn. If the obstruction is large, the intestines become unable to absorb food and digestive fluids. The result is severe abdominal pain and persistent, uncontrollable vomiting, which makes it impossible to eat normally. Consequently, intravenous feeding may be needed. Radner recalled: "I had almost a complete obstruction. Not only could my intestines not absorb food, they could not even absorb the natural secretions that my body produced. Bile would accumulate until I became nauseous and had to throw up. I could not eat. Only the intravenous feedings and fluids at night kept me alive."[8]

Obstruction of the kidneys can also be a problem. When an ovarian cancer tumor blocks the kidneys, urine backs up in the kidneys, which creates the frequent urge to urinate. Eventually, the kidneys may stop working entirely, which can be fatal.

Because cancer cells steal nourishment from healthy cells and make it difficult for affected cells to work properly, women with ovarian cancer also have problems with unexplained fatigue. Cindy Melancon, the founder of an ovarian cancer newsletter and a patient who died of the disease in 2003, explained: "[I] just could not get enough rest. Even with long naps over the weekends, I was still exhausted. . . . I only had energy to do something for about one to two hours, and then would have to rest for 30 to 45 minutes."[9]

Fluid in the Abdomen

Another problem caused by ovarian cancer is the buildup of fluids in the abdomen. This condition is known as ascites. It occurs when a tumor blocks the drainage of fluids through the lymphatic system. Instead, fluid gets trapped inside the abdomen, causing it to be become bloated and swollen. As a result, women with ovarian cancer often report a thickening around the waistline and an enlarged stomach. Sometimes, the stomach can become so enlarged that the woman appears pregnant. Although their stomach swells, ovarian cancer patients lose weight because dividing cancer cells consume nutrients meant for the body. Robin, the sister of an ovarian cancer survivor, recalls: "My sister was so bloated, she looked like she was four or five months pregnant. She even thought she was pregnant. She was really surprised when it turned out to be ovarian cancer."[10]

Individuals at Risk

Since the ovaries do not have a function until a female reaches puberty and starts menstruating, ovarian cells are inactive before puberty begins. Therefore, females who have not reached puberty cannot develop ovarian cancer. Thereafter, however, any woman can get ovarian cancer. But some—including women with a family history of ovarian cancer, middle-aged women who have never had children, women with a personal history of breast cancer, Jewish women of eastern European descent, and women over the age of sixty—are at greater risk.

About half of all cases of ovarian cancer occur in women over the age of sixty-five, with sixty-one being the average age at

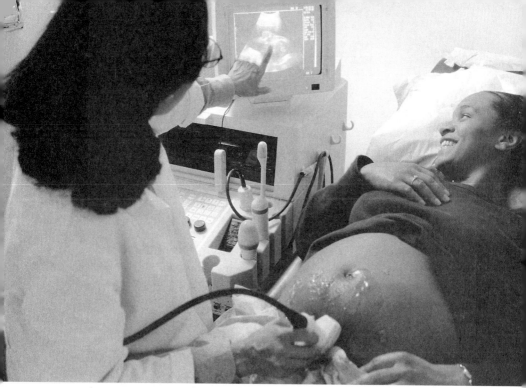

A pregnant women views an ultrasound image of her child. Studies show women who have had multiple pregnancies are less likely to develop ovarian cancer.

which women develop the disease. Older women may be at greater risk of developing ovarian cancer because over the course of their lives they have released more eggs than younger women. When a female reaches puberty, her ovaries release eggs each month. This continues until a woman reaches menopause. The eggs burst out of the walls of the ovaries into the fallopian tubes, where they may be fertilized. If they are not, they are shed from the body through menstruation. When the eggs are released, cells that line the ovarian walls are torn and must divide in order to repair the damage. Scientists theorize that the more often this happens, the greater the long-term toll on the ovaries and the more chances that an ovarian cell will mutate.

Ovarian cancer survivor and author Liz Tilberis describes this process:

> In every woman, every month from menarche to menopause [the start and end of menstruation], one egg enlarges and ruptures near the surface of the ovary, where it awaits its fate: It

may be fertilized by a congenial sperm and settle into the wall of the uterus on its way to becoming a baby or it may be sloughed off as part of a period. . . . But every time the egg blows through the ovary, the cells lining the surface have to divide and proliferate to fill in the hole left behind. It is in the normal, orderly repair of the hole that cells can run amok and cancerous changes begin.[11]

Monthly ovulation stops while a woman is pregnant. Since the risk of developing ovarian cancer increases the more often ovulation occurs, women who have never been pregnant are also at risk.

The BRCA Gene

Genetics also put some women at risk of developing ovarian cancer. According to the Ovarian Cancer National Alliance, 10 to 15 percent of all ovarian cancer cases are linked to heredity. Scientists theorize that some women inherit a tendency to develop ovarian cancer. Many, but not all, women with ovarian cancer inherit mutations on tumor suppressor genes called BRCA1 and BRCA2. Such mutations keep the genes from stopping ovarian cells from growing and dividing uncontrollably.

Women can inherit the defective gene from one or both parents. Thus, if this mutant gene runs in a woman's family, her relatives are likely to have had ovarian cancer, and she inherits a predisposition toward the disease.

Women with first-degree relatives, such as a mother or sister, who have had ovarian cancer have an increased chance of developing the disease. In the United States, the average woman has a 1.8 percent chance of developing ovarian cancer. This rises to 4 to 7 percent for a woman with a first-degree relative with the disease.

If two or more first-degree relatives have had ovarian cancer, those chances rise even more. According to the National Ovarian Cancer Coalition, being part of a family with a pattern of ovarian cancer raises a woman's chance of developing the disease to as high as 45 percent. If, in addition to first-degree relatives, other relatives such as a grandmother or an aunt also have had the disease, a woman's chances of developing the disease can rise to about 60 percent. Radner, for example, had four relatives with the disease. Robin also has a family history of ovarian cancer. She explains: "Both my grandmothers and my aunt died of ovarian cancer. My sister had ovarian cancer about thirteen years ago and survived. I know that puts me at risk."[12]

The Breast and Prostate Cancer Connection

Similarly, women who have had breast cancer are more likely to develop ovarian cancer. This is especially true if there is a family pattern of breast cancer or prostate cancer. Scientists theorize that this occurs because the same mutations in the BRCA genes that make individuals susceptible to developing ovarian cancer also predispose individuals to developing breast and prostate cancer.

Helen, an ovarian cancer survivor, explains: "My brother had prostate cancer about five years ago . . . and he found out that he had the mutation on the BRCA2 gene. . . . My first cousin who had stage 1 [the least severe] ovarian cancer over twenty years ago, also has the mutation. . . . I found out I had the mutation."[13]

Ethnic Links

Mutated BRCA genes are not common. The mutations are frequently found among certain ethnic groups, especially Jews of eastern European descent. This puts women in this group at risk. In fact, one in every forty Jews of eastern European descent has a BRCA gene mutation, compared to one in every eight hundred individuals in the general population. And 40 percent of Jewish women diagnosed with ovarian cancer have a BRCA gene mutation.

Because of this link, scientists say that the presence of BRCA mutations is an important indicator that an individual is predisposed to developing ovarian cancer. However, for reasons scientists do not undertstand, not everyone with a BRCA mutation will develop ovarian cancer and not all ovarian cancer patients have the mutation. But enough do for scientists to link the mutations to the disease. In fact, according to ovarian cancer experts

Gilda Radner

The person who is probably most responsible for making the public aware of the dangers of ovarian cancer is actress and comedian Gilda Radner, who died of the disease in 1989 at the age of forty-two.

Radner was born in Detroit, Michigan. From childhood, she knew she wanted to be an actress. She first performed professionally in a production of the rock opera *Godspell* in Toronto, Ontario, in the early 1970s. While living in Toronto, she joined the Second City Improvisational Troupe, which also featured comedians John Candy, John Belushi, and Dan Aykroyd. But she is probably best known for her role on *Saturday Night Live*.

Radner was one of the original cast members of the show, which began in 1975. She became famous for the many characters she created such as Roseanne Rosannadanna, Lisa Lupner, and Emily Litella. During her years on the show, she received three Emmy Award nominations.

In 1984 she married actor and comedian Gene Wilder. They made a number of movies together, including *The Woman in Red* and *Haunted Honeymoon*.

In 1986 Radner was diagnosed with ovarian cancer. For almost three years she fought the disease. At the same time, she wrote *It's Always Something*, a book detailing her life with ovarian cancer.

In the book's introduction she explained:

> On October 21, 1986, I was diagnosed with ovarian cancer. Suddenly I had to spend all my time getting well. I was fighting for my life against cancer, a more lethal foe than even the interior decorator. The book has turned out a bit differently from what I had intended. It's a book about illness, doctors and hospitals. . . . Cancer is probably the most unfunny thing in the world, but I'm a comedienne, and even cancer couldn't stop me from seeing humor in what I went through. So, I am sharing with you what I call a seriously funny book, one that

confirms my father's favorite expression about life, "It's always something."

After her death, her friends and family founded Gilda's Club, a national network of cancer support centers that offer counseling, education, and support programs for cancer patients and their families.

Comedian Gilda Radner inspired thousands of fellow ovarian cancer patients with her humor during her three-year battle with the disease that took her life in 1989.

Kristine Conner and Lauren Langford, scientists estimate that the presence of a BRCA1 mutation increases a woman's chance of developing ovarian cancer from 1.8 percent to as high as 60 percent. Similarly, the presence of the BRCA2 mutation increases an individual's risk to as high as 25 percent.

Sue, who carries the BRCA2 mutation, explains:

> When you test positive for an inherited mutation, you are diagnosed not with a disease but with a percentage—a risk of getting cancer that is higher than the general population's risk. . . . If you've never had cancer you're . . . a cancer pre-vivor, which stands for survivor of a predisposition to cancer. . . . Even if you have already had breast or ovarian cancer, you know that the mutation increases your risk for the other diagnosis.[14]

Decreasing the Risk

Because heredity and the presence of BRCA mutations play a key role in predisposing an individual to developing ovarian cancer, some women undergo genetic testing to ascertain whether they have BRCA mutations. This is a simple test in which a blood sample is analyzed for the presence of BRCA gene mutations. If a mutation is found, it does not guarantee that the individual will develop ovarian cancer, but it lets her know that she is at high risk. She can then take steps to help prevent ovarian cancer from occurring, including increased screening and surveillance, taking oral contraceptives, avoiding fertility drugs and hormone replacement therapy, and undergoing preventive surgery.

Increased screening and surveillance involves biannual medical exams that include a pelvic exam, a blood test, and an ultrasound. These tests are not normally administered to the general population. Although these tests cannot lower a woman's risk of developing the disease, they can help to detect the disease before it can metastasize, which can save a person's life. Indeed, 85 to 90 percent of ovarian cancer cases that are discovered before the disease metastasizes are cured.

On the other hand, taking oral contraceptives (called birth control pills or the Pill) does appear to lower a woman's risk of developing ovarian cancer. The reason for this is that chemicals in oral contraceptives prevent ovulation in order to prevent pregnancy. A 2000 study by the National Cancer Institute's Breast and Gynecologic Cancer Research Group in Bethesda, Maryland, found that taking oral contraceptives for five years decreases a woman's risk of developing ovarian cancer by as much as 50 percent. Cindy, an ovarian cancer survivor with the BRCA mutation, explains the steps her high-risk teenage daughter is taking: "The doctor recommends that she have intense screenings starting at age 30. It's also been recommended that she go on The Pill. . . . She understands that this might make a difference in her risk for ovarian cancer."[15]

Conversely, high-risk individuals often avoid taking fertility drugs. Although there is no conclusive evidence that these drugs

Cancer specialists recommend that women over sixty with a family history of ovarian cancer have biannual ultrasound screenings to give early warning of the disease.

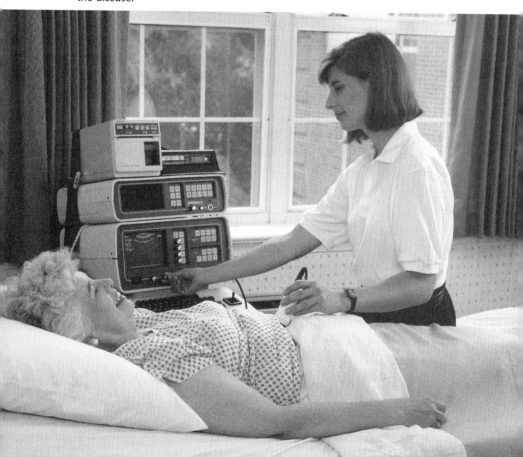

promote ovarian cancer, they do stimulate ovulation. Similarly, hormone replacement therapy, which is often administered to help women cope with the symptoms of menopause, may also increase an individual's risk of developing ovarian cancer. Once again, this theory has not been proven, but research suggests that it is likely. According to a 2004 article in the *Gilda Radner Familial Ovarian Cancer Registry Newsletter* that analyzes the results of various studies, hormone therapy raises a woman's risk of developing ovarian cancer by close to 60 percent. Scientists are unclear why hormone replacement therapy may increase a woman's risk of developing ovarian cancer, but they theorize that excessive estrogen may encourage the growth of malignant ovarian tumors.

Preventive Surgery

A woman who has tested positive for a BRCA mutation and has a strong family history of ovarian cancer may choose to have preventive surgery in an effort to keep herself free of ovarian cancer. Some undergo a radical hysterectomy, in which their ovaries, fallopian tubes, uterus, and cervix are removed. Others undergo a prophylactic (preventive) oophorectomy, in which just the ovaries are removed. Both operations present health risks, and once a woman has had these organs removed she can no longer become pregnant.

Despite these drawbacks, the Gilda Radner Familial Ovarian Cancer Registry, which provides help for individuals with a family history of ovarian cancer, recommends that women with two or more first-degree relatives with ovarian cancer undergo preventive surgery. Since this surgery can be risky and keeps a woman from bearing children—and since a woman with first-degree relatives with ovarian cancer will not necessarily develop the disease herself—taking such a step is a drastic measure. But it provides many high-risk women with the knowledge that they are doing everything possible to lessen their chances of developing ovarian cancer. Nina, a woman with the BRCA2 mutation and a family history of ovarian cancer, explains: "I decided to undergo a prophylactic oophorectomy. I was 44 at the time and was finished having kids. . . . To me, having the surgery was a no-brainer, since it significantly reduced my chances of getting ovarian cancer. . . . I am so glad that I had the surgery, and I feel that the peace of mind was well worth the choice of having my ovaries removed."[16]

Clearly, opting to have healthy organs removed is an extreme measure. On the other hand, ovarian cancer is a life-threatening disease. For women at high risk, taking preventive steps can help reduce the likelihood of ovarian cancer developing and can save lives.

Chapter 2

Confusing Symptoms and a Difficult Diagnosis

O VARIAN CANCER SYMPTOMS are deceiving. Similar symptoms often affect healthy women at some point in their lives. Moreover, a number of other ailments have comparable symptoms. This makes it easy to confuse ovarian cancer symptoms with those of other diseases.

Diagnosis, too, is difficult. There is no reliable test that can absolutely identify the presence of the disease. Only surgery and analysis of the tissue removed can provide a reliable diagnosis.

Confusing Symptoms

Ovarian cancer symptoms are vague. They include constipation; heartburn; indigestion; a frequent, urgent need to urinate; abdominal swelling and bloating; unexplained weight loss; fatigue; pain in the pelvis, back, or abdomen; abnormal vaginal bleeding or discharge; and pain during intercourse. These symptoms do not always cluster together, nor are they specific to ovarian cancer. When they appear separately, they are often mistaken for other problems. Frequently, they are attributed to aging, stress, or menopause. Fatigue, pain in the pelvis, abnormal bleeding, and pain during intercourse, in particular, are often symptoms of menopause. Unexplained fatigue, pain, and weight loss can be signs of stress; while constipation and abdominal bloating and swelling sometimes accompany aging. This was the case for Marian's mother. Marian recalls:

30

Eleven years ago, my mother, 65, was having abdominal bloating, fullness and discomfort. As a petite woman, her clothes no longer seemed to fit around her waist. She kept saying, "Look at my stomach! I don't have a stomach like this." For six months she was in and out of doctors' offices. . . . She heard suggestions like try sit-ups, you know you are no spring chicken, [and] what do you expect your waist to be like at your age?[17]

Ovarian cancer symptoms are also frequently confused with less serious, more common conditions such as urinary tract infection, irritable bowel syndrome, or chronic fatigue syndrome. Many women with symptoms such as constipation, indigestion, fatigue, a bloated feeling, back pain, or a frequent urge to urinate do not seek medical attention. Instead, they blame their problems on something they ate, stress, or a urinary tract infection, conditions they believe can be treated without a doctor's care.

Women who wake with abdominal cramps rarely suspect them to be symptoms of ovarian cancer. Many of the cancer's symptoms are not specific to the disease.

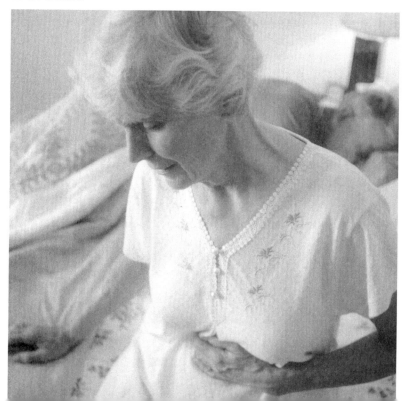

Study Pinpoints Three Symptoms of Early-Stage Ovarian Cancer

Lack of clearly identifiable symptoms is one reason ovarian cancer is hard to diagnose. A 2004 study conducted by Barbara Goff of the University of Washington sought to determine if women with ovarian cancer were more likely than healthy women to report certain symptoms. The survey questioned 1,709 healthy women and 128 women awaiting surgery for pelvic tumors linked to early-stage ovarian cancer. The survey found a cluster of three symptoms common to all the women with ovarian cancer: a swollen abdomen, a bloated feeling, and frequent, urgent urination.

The survey is important because awareness of this cluster of symptoms should help alert women and their doctors to the possibility of ovarian cancer. This should make it more likely to catch ovarian cancer at an early stage. An article by Lindsey Tanner appearing in the *Albuquerque Journal* describes what Goff found:

> All three symptoms were found in 43 percent of women later diagnosed with ovarian cancer, but in just 8 percent of women without the disease.

> Women with ovarian cancer also were more likely than others to report that symptoms began within the preceding several weeks rather than several months or years earlier. Their symptoms also were more likely to be severe and to occur as often as every day or most days.

> The cluster of symptoms occurred in women in early-stage disease and those with more advanced cases. . . .

> The three symptoms, if recent and persistent, should indicate to doctors that these women "have to be evaluated instead of just giving them relief for bloating, or saying 'That's normal,'" said Dr. Carmen Rodriguez of the American Cancer Society.

Melancon noted:

> I found myself needing to urinate again several minutes after I
> thought I had emptied my bladder. But we had just been to the
> Gulf Coast and I believed I had picked up a little bladder irri-
> tation from the water down there. . . . The rest of my symptoms
> I put down to simple stress and a hectic schedule. . . . In my
> mind there were no unusual symptoms that could possibly be
> related to the mass in my abdomen. After all, stress and fatigue
> are a normal part of a busy woman's life.[18]

When individuals do seek medical treatment, ovarian cancer
symptoms are often misdiagnosed. Anita, who cared for her
mother during her fight against ovarian cancer, explains: "One
problem is the symptoms are very vague. You can have most of
the symptoms for many reasons. Mother was having trouble
with constipation, and they diagnosed her with irritable bowel
syndrome. Then she had abnormal bleeding and they thought
there was a problem in her uterus. The symptoms are not always
tied together."[19]

Charissa had a similar experience. Her primary symptom, frequent urination, resembled that of a urinary tract infection. She
recalls: "I decided to pay a visit to my friendly M.D. . . . I asked
him to test me for a bladder infection and to be on the safe side,
a pregnancy test. Both were negative. . . . So he patted me on the
head, [and] told me it was hormonal."[20]

Herbert Kotz is a National Cancer Institute gynecologic oncologist, that is, a doctor who specializes in treating cancer of a woman's
reproductive system. He explains why such problems occur:

> The main problem is that these symptoms often mimic the nor-
> mal sensations that every human being has at one time or an-
> other—gas pressure, feeling tired, feeling bloated. If a woman
> goes to her physician and she feels tired or bloated, ovarian
> cancer won't be the first thing that comes to mind. And it's
> hard to alert the physician to think of ovarian cancer when a
> mild disorder of the intestinal tract could cause the same
> symptoms and is much more likely.[21]

With such vague and confusing symptoms, it is not surprising that about 75 percent of ovarian cancer cases are not detected until the cancer has spread. Unfortunately, the longer it takes to diagnose ovarian cancer, the more time the cancer has to grow and metastasize.

A Pelvic Exam

Despite these problems, when a patient exhibits a combination of symptoms, particularly abdominal swelling and bloating and an urgent, frequent need to urinate, ovarian cancer is suspected. So, too, is the disease suspected if the patient's symptoms are persistent, or if the patient is high risk. However, because the ovaries are located deep in the pelvis, there is no reliable test to positively diagnose the disease. Exploratory surgery, in which ovarian cells are removed and analyzed for the presence of cancer, is the only conclusive way to diagnose ovarian cancer. Such surgery is a major procedure. Consequently, it is not administered unless other, less conclusive procedures point to ovarian cancer. These procedures include a pelvic exam, a blood test, and imaging tests.

A gynecologist usually administers a pelvic exam. During a pelvic exam, the doctor feels the patient's abdomen, looking for hardness or lumps, which indicate the ovaries may be swollen or a tumor may be present. Then the doctor feels inside the patient's vagina while pressing on her abdomen, in an effort to find any swelling or unusual growth leading from the surface of the ovaries to the abdomen. Finally, the doctor feels inside the patient's vagina and rectum at the same time, in an effort to find any abnormal growth leading from the ovaries to the rectum. However, because of the size and location of the ovaries, it is not always possible for the doctor to locate abnormalities in this way. But a pelvic exam is a good first step in gathering evidence of ovarian cancer.

A pelvic exam was the first step in diagnosing Charissa. She recalls that during a pelvic exam the gynecologist "palpitated my abdomen and immediately asked, 'you had a pregnancy test?' I assured him I did and knew I was not pregnant. He said I had a

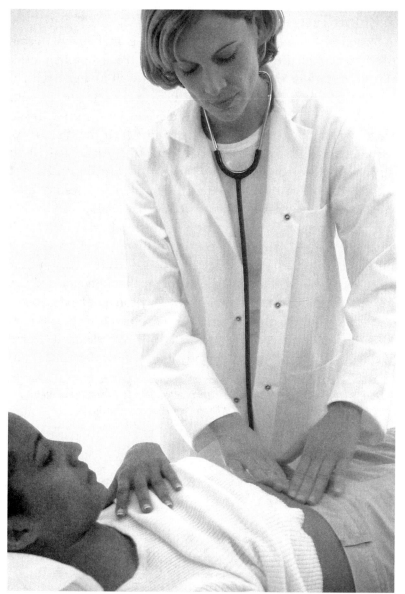

Gynecologists can detect abnormalities during pelvic exams when they palpitate a woman's abdomen to feel the shape and size of her internal organs.

mass the size of a 4 month fetus."[22] Such a mass may be a benign tumor or a liquid-filled growth called a cyst. Charissa's mass turned out to be an ovarian cancer tumor.

A Blood Test

A blood test that measures levels of CA-125 is another tool doctors use to find evidence of ovarian cancer. CA-125 is a protein found on the surface of ovarian cancer cells, as well as other cells. In healthy people, CA-125 levels are generally between zero and thirty-five. CA-125 levels are usually elevated in women with late-stage ovarian cancer, especially those in which the disease has metastasized. For reasons scientists do not understand, only about 40 percent of women in the early stages of ovarian cancer have elevated CA-125 levels. Consequently, CA-125 test results often come back negative even when a woman has ovarian cancer.

Other problems arise because CA-125 levels also increase in pregnant women, during menstruation, and in the presence of other problems in the reproductive organs, such as a benign ovarian tumor or an inflammation. Therefore, although elevated CA-125 levels can indicate ovarian cancer, they can also be deceiving.

Because of these drawbacks, a CA-125 blood test alone is not a reliable ovarian cancer screening tool. However, elevated CA-125 levels do alert the doctor to the possibility of ovarian cancer, and

Ovarian cancer specialists often ask their colleagues for a second opinion when their patient's X-ray and CAT scan results are inconclusive.

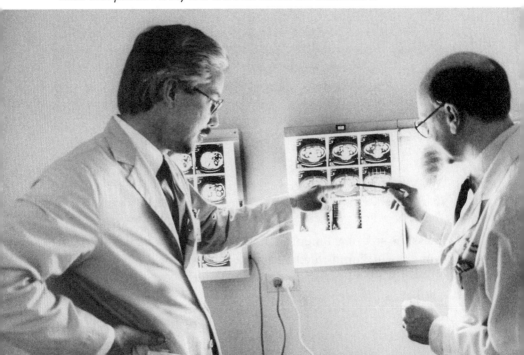

when a CA-125 blood test is combined with a pelvic exam and imaging tests, it does have great value.

Imaging Tests

If CA-125 levels are high, or if the doctor detects an abnormal mass during the pelvic exam, an imaging test is administered. One common test is a transvaginal ultrasound, in which sound waves are processed by a computer to create a picture of a woman's ovaries. During this test, a small sound-producing device, which is attached to a computer, is placed inside the patient's vagina. Similar in size and shape to a tampon, the device produces sound waves that bounce off the ovary and back to the probe. The reflected sound waves form a pattern, which a computer program translates into an image on a computer monitor of the patient's ovaries. If there is an abnormal growth present, it will usually show up on this picture.

Ovarian cancer survivor Christina recalls:

> While having the ultrasound, I knew it wasn't routine, as the technician took about a thousand pictures and gave only vague answers to my simple questions. After getting dressed, I reported as requested to the gynecologist . . . and he immediately started to look at the slides. . . . [He] explained that I had complex masses on both ovaries and that I would need surgery as soon as possible. He avoided the word "cancer" until I used it.[23]

Computerized axial tomography, or a CAT scan, may also be administered. Like an X-ray, a CAT scan takes pictures of the body. But instead of taking pictures of bones, it takes three-dimensional pictures of soft tissues. During a CAT scan, the patient lies on a moving table that passes through an imaging machine, which takes a detailed picture of specific internal organs. In the case of ovarian cancer, pictures are taken of all the organs in the patient's midsection. As in an ultrasound, the pictures are viewed on a computer monitor. Tumors appear as dark masses.

If a tumor is detected, the doctor can use the CAT scan and ultrasound pictures to determine the location and size of the tumor. However, the detection of an abnormal growth during imaging tests does not conclusively prove that the patient has ovarian cancer. The growth may be a benign tumor or a cyst. Only surgery can determine whether or not the tumor is cancerous.

A Surgical Diagnosis

If the pelvic exam, blood test, and imaging results point to ovarian cancer, exploratory surgery is needed to confirm the diagnosis. It acts as both a means of diagnosis and, if ovarian cancer is found, a form of treatment.

Surgery to diagnose ovarian cancer is known as a laparotomy. Before the surgery begins, the patient is sedated. Once she is asleep, a vertical incision is made from just below her belly button down to her pubic bone. The skin is then pulled back and the doctor examines the patient's ovaries, pelvis, abdomen, and liver for suspected tumors. If a tumor is found, the doctor removes the whole tumor, being careful not to break it. This is important because if a cancerous tumor is broken open, cancer cells can spill out and spread to other parts of the body. This is known as seeding.

Besides inspecting the patient's ovaries and removing tumors there, the doctor visually examines adjacent organs in the patient's midsection. Tumors and random tissue samples from the patient's abdomen, pelvis, diaphragm, pelvic lymph nodes, and liver are removed. Since ovarian cancer commonly spreads to these nearby body parts, this is done to determine whether they have been infected with cancer.

Once the tumor and surrounding tissue are removed, they are sent to a laboratory where a biopsy is performed. Here, a doctor known as a pathologist examines the tumor and surrounding tissue under a microscope. By looking for evidence that the cells are dividing and for abnormal changes in the cells' shape, the pathologist is able to determine whether the cells from the biopsy are malignant or benign. The pathologist's report is then sent back to the operating room. If the tumor is benign, the incision is closed and no further surgery is required. If the tumor is malignant, additional surgery is performed immediately in an effort to rid the body of cancer. The patient and her family are informed of the results once the surgery is completed.

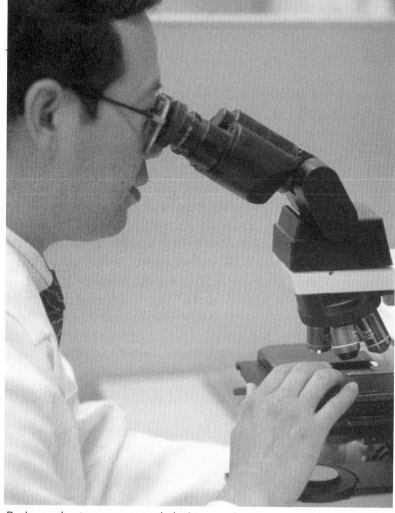

During exploratory surgery, pathologists examine tissue samples extracted by the surgeon to determine if the cells are benign or malignant.

Ramona, an ovarian cancer survivor, talks about her experience:

The day of the surgery came about. I did not feel nervous or uneasy but I did have a feeling of dread, call it, woman's intuition. I awoke not being able to move as much as I thought I would. In the background I could hear the nurses speaking in hushed tones, "she is so young." I knew they were speaking of me. As I was placed in my room, I could hear my family coming in and out and speaking to me, telling me everything was going to be okay. . . . I remember looking at my husband, asking him how the surgery had gone, only to be answered with sad looking eyes and a response I did not want to hear.[24]

Determining Which Cells Are Malignant

Once the pathologist confirms the presence of ovarian cancer, he or she identifies the type of ovarian cells affected. There are three different types of ovarian cells: epithelial cells, germ cells, and sex cord-stromal cells. Each is located in a different part of the ovary and each has a different function. Cancer can develop in all three types of cells, but because all three types are not treated in the same manner, it is important that the cell type be identified.

Epithelial ovarian cancer arises in the cells that line and cover the surface of the ovaries. Since epithelial cells are shed every time a woman ovulates, and must divide in order to replace themselves, the chance of these cells mutating is high. Consequently, epithelial cancer is the most common type of ovarian cancer, comprising 90

Cancer specialists used a scanning electron micrograph to photograph these malignant cancerous cells found on the surface of the ovaries.

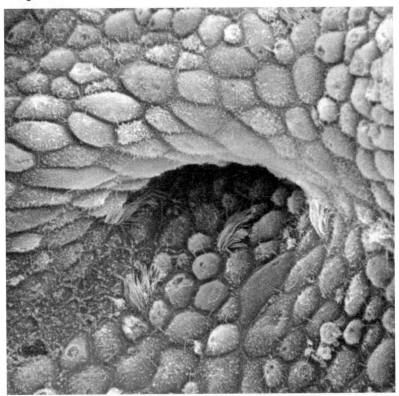

percent of all ovarian cancer cases diagnosed each year. And since cancer cells are more likely to spread during menstruation, epithelial cancer metastasizes more rapidly than germ or sex cord-stromal cell cancer. This makes it more difficult to treat.

Germ cell cancer and sex cord-stromal cell cancer are less common. Only 3 percent of all ovarian cancer cases arise in the germ cells, which are the cells that produce eggs. Five to 7 percent of ovarian cancer cases affect sex cord-stromal cells. These cells are located in connective tissue that surrounds the ovaries. Unlike epithelial tumors, which are most likely to occur in older women, sex cord-stromal cell tumors arise in women of all ages who have begun to menstruate, while germ cell tumors usually develop in teens and women in their twenties. Scientists do not know why this is so.

Sex cord-stromal cell tumors grow and spread very slowly. Germ cell tumors are more aggressive than sex cord-stromal cell tumors, but do not spread rapidly. Both forms of ovarian cancer usually respond well to treatment and are less likely to return than epithelial cancer. In fact, approximately 95 percent of germ cell and sex cord-stromal cell cancers are cured. Betsy, a germ cell cancer survivor, recalls:

> Ten and a half years ago, I was an active 17 year old high school student, the editor of the school's newspaper, and captain of the girls' swim team when I was diagnosed with ovarian cancer. When my abdomen began to distend (and I assured my parents I could not be pregnant) I was taken to an OB/GYN [an obstetrician/gynecologist]. Three days later my GYN/ONC [gynecologic oncologist] removed a 5.5 pound tumor, the size of a volleyball from my right ovary. . . . I was diagnosed with . . . a Germ Cell Tumor. . . . I have a 95% cure rate, and have never had a recurrence. I have since married and have gone on to have two wonderful, healthy children with hopes to have more.[25]

Cancer Stage and Grade

In addition to determining the type of ovarian cancer present, the pathologist also establishes the stage and grade of the cancer. The stage of the cancer describes the location of the cancer, whether it has spread, and, if it has, how far away from the ovaries it extends. To make this determination, the pathologist examines cells taken from the patient's abdomen, pelvis, diaphragm, pelvic lymph nodes, and liver during exploratory surgery. Then, depending on what is found, the cancer is classified as stage I, II, III, or IV.

Stage I indicates that the cancer is confined to the ovaries, and has not spread to other organs. Twenty percent of ovarian cancer cases are diagnosed in stage I. Stage II means cancer cells have spread beyond the ovaries but are contained within the pelvis. In this case, cancer cells may be found in the uterus, vagina, bladder, and large intestine. Ten percent of all ovarian cancer cases are diagnosed in stage II. However, once ovarian cancer starts to metastasize the cancer spreads beyond the pelvis rapidly, so few untreated cases of ovarian cancer remain at stage II for long. That is why 60 percent of all ovarian cancer cases are diagnosed at stage III. In stage III the cancer has spread beyond the pelvis and affects the stomach, small intestine, and nearby lymph nodes, but not the liver. When cancer cells have spread to the liver, and possibly to the lungs and brain, the disease has reached stage IV. Since these organs are vital for life, once cancer spreads to them the patient's chance of long-term survival decreases. Ten percent of ovarian cancer cases are diagnosed in stage IV.

Next, the grade of cancer is established. This describes how greatly the cancer cells differ from normal cells. To make this determination the pathologist compares the shape and growth rate of cancer cells from the biopsy to normal cells. Normal cells generally have regular borders and grow slowly, whereas cancer cells have jagged or irregular borders and grow quickly. Depending on how much the cells from the biopsy differ from normal cells, the cancer cells are given a grade from 1 to 3. Grade 1 cells resemble normal cells, and are called well differentiated. They divide slowly and are less likely to spread outside the ovaries than higher-grade cells. Grade 2 cells look more abnormal. They are said to be moderately differentiated and are more aggressive than grade 1 cells. Grade 3 cells are the least like normal cells. They are poorly differentiated, and are likely to spread rapidly.

Johanna's Law

Since ovarian cancer is frequently mistaken for other illnesses and many people are unaware what the disease's symptoms are, many women are not diagnosed until the cancer has spread. In order to increase awareness of what to look for, a bill known as Johanna's Law has been proposed. The law provides funding for federal education to provide women and health care professionals with the latest information about the symptoms of ovarian cancer and other gynecologic cancers.

In her May 2004 *Jewish Week* article, Francesca Lunzer Kritz discusses the bill:

> It's called Johanna's Law. And if it passes, perhaps tens of thousands of women could owe their lives to Johanna Silver Gordon, and her sister, Sheryl Silver. Johanna Gordon was diagnosed with ovarian cancer in 1996, after she and her doctors failed to recognize signs of the cancer until it was too late. When she was finally diagnosed, Johanna's cancer was at stage III—very advanced.

> "Johanna was a vigorously healthy and health conscious woman," Johanna's younger sister Sheryl Silver said. "Unfortunately, what my sister didn't know about gynecological cancer proved deadly."

> Common symptoms of ovarian cancer include persistent heartburn and abdominal bloating. "Not knowing those basic facts led to a delay in her diagnosis," says Silver. She had no idea her symptoms were due to cancer and needed the attention of a gynecologic oncologist.

> In 2002, Silver began writing articles about gynecologic cancers to educate the public and soon decided federal legislation was the best way to inform women about these diseases. She took her sister's story to Capitol Hill and proposed such legislation to Rep. Sander Levin, Johanna's congressman for many years. It is called Johanna's Law: The Gynecologic Cancer Education and Awareness Act (H.R. 3438) and it is currently pending.

Stages of Ovarian Cancer

Stage	Extent of Cancer	5-Year Survival Rate
I	Cancer cells are limited to the ovaries.	95%
II	Cancer cells are in one or both ovaries with extension to the pelvic region.	65%
III	Cancer cells have spread beyond pelvis, possibly to stomach, small intestine, and nearby lymph nodes. Sixty percent of all cases are diagnosed at this stage.	15–30%
IV	Cancer cells have spread to the liver, and possibly to lungs and brain.	0–20%

Making a Prognosis

Once the type of cells, stage, and grade of cancer are established, the doctor uses this information to make a prognosis. This is an estimate of how likely the patient is to be cured, or what the patient's long-term survival chances are. It is based on statistics on how well other patients of the same age with the same type, stage, and grade of cancer have fared. For instance, since most young patients with stage I, grade 1, germ cell ovarian cancer are cured, the prognosis for such an individual is 95 percent chance of being cured. Indeed, the prognosis for all types of stage I, grade 1 ovarian cancer is excellent. Generally, the higher the grade and stage of cancer, especially in epithelial cancer, and the older the patient, the poorer the prognosis. However, 50 percent of all women with ovarian cancer, no matter their age, type, stage, or grade of cancer, survive at least five years after diagnosis. Nan, an ovarian cancer survivor, explains:

> Stage IV is not an immediate death sentence, and you have to keep reminding yourself that each individual is different and you cannot let your life be ruled by statistics. Whenever I told

people I was stage IV, everyone looked sad and assumed I was going to just get worse and worse and then die, that's it. My department at work even had a death counselor in to talk to my colleagues one week after my diagnosis. After a year, I am back at work full-time and people are surprised.[26]

Indeed, because ovarian cancer symptoms are confusing and making a diagnosis is difficult, many women are not diagnosed until their cancer has reached stage III or IV, which worsens their prognosis. But a prognosis is only a prediction. Once a diagnosis is made, steps can be taken to increase an individual's chances of long-term survival.

Chapter 3

Conventional and Complementary Treatment

O NCE A SURGICAL diagnosis of ovarian cancer is made, treatment begins while the patient is still in surgery. In most cases, when the patient recovers from surgery she is administered chemotherapy, which is a combination of drugs taken intravenously to keep cells from dividing. Chemotherapy can have a number of unpleasant side effects. To combat these side effects and to make chemotherapy more effective, many individuals augment chemotherapy with alternative treatments. Once treatment is over, some patients are cured. Others experience periods of remission and recurrences of ovarian cancers. These individuals require further treatment.

Surgical Treatment

Once cells are biopsied and the type, stage, and grade of cancer is established, surgical treatment begins. Surgical treatment for ovarian cancer is known as debulking. It involves the surgical removal of cancer from the body. If the cancer is in stage I, the doctor removes the patient's fallopian tubes, ovaries, and uterus. This is known as a hysterectomy.

Having a hysterectomy makes a woman infertile. This is especially hard for young women who want to be able to have a baby in the future. If a woman is in stage I and evidence of cancer is found in only one ovary, fertility-sparing surgery may be performed. In this procedure, the uninvolved ovary, one fallopian tube, and the

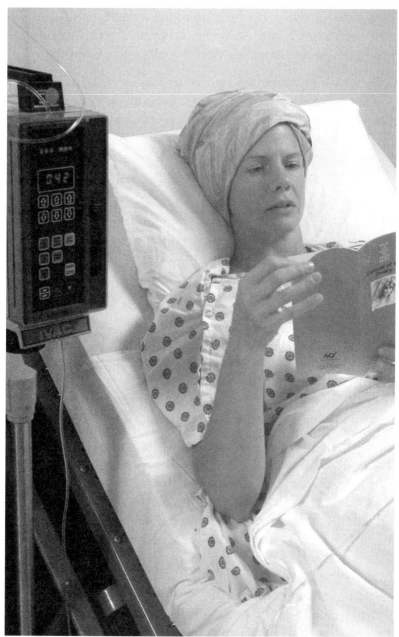

Ovarian cancer patients are often treated with chemotherapy, which is administered intravenously. The effectiveness of the treatments varies widely between patients.

uterus are left intact. However, since the reproductive organs that are not removed may contain microscopic ovarian cancer cells, the cancer is likely to come back. April describes her experience:

> Because the tumor in my right ovary was early-stage . . . I had a good prognosis and was able to keep my left ovary. A few years later, I was lucky enough to give birth to my daughter. The cancer did come back in just the past year. . . . This time around I had the full surgery. . . . I was just glad I had the window during which I was able to have a child.[27]

When the cancer is more aggressive or when both ovaries are involved, the threat to the patient's life makes fertility-sparing surgery unwise. In these cases, a hysterectomy is performed. Loss of fertility can be devastating. Author and ovarian cancer survivor Andrea Gibbs Brown explains:

> It took me a long time to mourn the loss of fertility. This has been hard on us as a couple because we so greatly wanted children. We have talked about adoption but have decided for the time being to leave it be. Time has helped us to accept these changes and to look forward instead of looking back to what could have been. Psychotherapy . . . has helped us. But it remains poignant to remember what was lost.[28]

Further Debulking

When the cancer is more advanced, debulking is more extensive. In advanced cases, parts of the intestines, rectum, bladder, diaphragm, abdomen, liver, kidney, and spleen, as well as pelvic lymph nodes that show evidence of cancer, may be removed. When possible, the remaining portions of the organs are reattached. Ramona explains: "The doctor performed a hysterectomy. . . . Seventy percent of my liver was removed, my right adrenal gland was removed, a mass behind my spleen was removed, and my gallbladder was removed, and several tiny masses from my abdomen were removed."[29]

The goal of debulking is to remove all cancer cells from the body. When this is not possible, such as in cases in which the cancer is widespread or is infecting a larger portion of an organ than can be removed without affecting the patient's health and quality of life, the doctor removes as many cancer cells as possible. In general, the more cancer that is removed the better the patient's prognosis. Johns Hopkins University gynecologic oncologist Edward Trimble explains: "Gynecologic oncologists share the belief—they are trained according to this belief—that you must make the maximal effort to remove all of the cancer that's visible to the naked eye. If you can't do that safely then you need to remove as much as you can, but not put the patient at such great risk that the risks of surgery begin to outweigh the benefits."[30] When the risks of surgery outweigh the benefits, the organs are not removed. Instead, these patients are administered more cycles of chemotherapy than the norm.

But no matter how extensive the debulking, any type of surgery is risky. Patients can develop dangerous infections or experience allergic reactions to anesthesia. And until surgical wounds heal, patients often feel sore and achy.

If cancerous cells spread from the ovaries to the uterus (pictured), surgeons perform a hysterectomy in order to remove the infected organ.

Getting Ready for Chemotherapy

If the patient is completely debulked and there are no visible signs of cancer remaining in her body, treatment of stage I epithelial cancer, all stages of sex cord-stromal cancer, and stage I and II germ cell tumors ends with surgery. For individuals with more advanced stage germ cell or epithelial tumors, chemotherapy is administered. These particular classifications of ovarian cancer are aggressive. This means that microscopic cancer cells, invisible to the naked eye, may have spread to areas that debulking missed. In order to destroy these cells, and hopefully cure the cancer, chemotherapy is administered.

Chemotherapy keeps cells from dividing. If a cell cannot divide, it will die. Because cancer cells divide rapidly, they are especially vulnerable to chemotherapy. Some chemotherapy drugs used to treat ovarian cancer, such as carboplatin, create breaks in

A team of nurses implants a port-a-catheter under the skin into a patient's chest through which intravenous chemotherapy drugs can be administered.

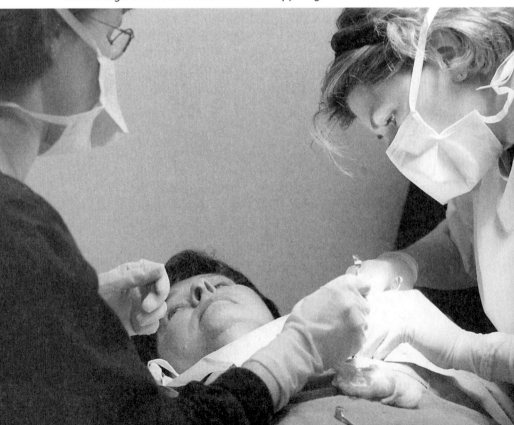

a cell's DNA (the genetic substance that is needed in order for cells to replicate). This prevents the cell from dividing and growing. Other drugs called mitotic inhibitors interrupt cells while they are dividing by blocking microtubules, tiny structures found in all cells that are needed for cell division. The end result is the destruction of cancer cells. However, normal cells are also destroyed in the process. Most vulnerable are healthy cells in an individual's bone marrow, hair follicles, and digestive tract, because these cells divide more rapidly than other cells.

Because chemotherapy is administered intravenously, requiring patients to endure at least eighteen needle sticks—and usually more—during the course of chemotherapy, many patients are fitted with a port-a-catheter before chemotherapy begins. This is a plastic device that resembles a small bottle with a wire neck. The bottle is implanted into a patient's chest, where it lies flat. The wire neck is inserted into a central vein. The port has a small hole that sticks out of the skin. Intravenous medication can be administered to the body through the hole. This allows the patient to avoid frequent needle sticks. Anita explains: "Having a port-a-catheter really did help my mother because she really didn't like needles. With the port, they could go in, access it with a special needle that easily goes into the port rather than the skin, and that's it, no needle sticks."[31]

In addition, before chemotherapy begins, the patient's CA-125 level is measured. It is then monitored and compared while chemotherapy is taking place. If CA-125 levels fall during the course of chemotherapy, it is a positive, although not conclusive, sign that the treatment is working.

Because adequate red and white blood cells are needed to combat infection and fatigue, these are also checked before and during chemotherapy. And before patients undergo chemotherapy, drugs called steroids are administered. Steroids prevent the patient from developing an allergic reaction to the chemotherapy medicine, as well as lessening any other adverse reactions. Radner explained: "The steroids masked the side effects of the chemotherapy. As long as I was on them, I was able to watch television, do needlepoint, and be fairly peaceful."[32]

Chemotherapy

Chemotherapy is usually administered once a week for three weeks, followed by a three-week break. Most patients are given six cycles. Some stage IV patients are given eight cycles. This is because cancer is more aggressive and abundant in stage IV, so more doses of chemotherapy may be needed to destroy it.

Generally, each treatment takes anywhere from three to six hours. Chemotherapy usually takes place in a special hospital suite equipped with comfortable recliner chairs. The patient relaxes in the chair while an intravenous bag drips medicine into her port-a-catheter. Nurses monitor the process. Most rooms are equipped with a television and reading material. Usually a number of patients receive chemotherapy at the same time. Individuals often nap, chat, or visit with friends and family members who accompany them. Lynne describes her experience:

> Chemotherapy wasn't all I expected. I thought I would see very sick people getting even sicker from chemotherapy. Instead I saw all these people eating their lunch, . . . watching TV, listening to CDs, reading, talking with family members, napping, all while these drugs were dripping into them. It was just so strange. I also thought I would be able to feel the chemotherapy going into me, but that wasn't the case. Really, it was just plain boring![33]

Remission and Recurrence

Chemotherapy does not work well on every patient, but approximately 70 to 80 percent of ovarian cancer patients respond well to it. It cures about 30 percent of ovarian cancer cases. Other patients remain cancer free for a period of months or years, but then ovarian cancer recurs. This may seem strange, since these patients have had their ovaries and adjacent organs removed. But ovarian cancer cells can spread from the ovaries to other parts of the body, where they can hide in remaining tissues. These cells that resist the effects of chemotherapy eventually return as ovarian cancer.

Doctors have no way of telling whether this will happen. Therefore, all patients who successfully complete chemotherapy are said to be in remission. That means that there is no evidence of cancer, but the disease may recur. Jean explains: "In my mind after I was treated the cancer was gone for good. Only later on

Clinical Trials

Clinical trials are research studies involving human subjects rather than laboratory specimens or animals. Some clinical trials test the effectiveness of new medications. Other trials analyze how well new doses of proven medications, new combinations of medications, or new ways to administer medication help combat ovarian cancer.

Drug manufacturers, hospitals, and research institutes sponsor most clinical trials. In order for a particular treatment to be used in a clinical trial, the treatment must first be carefully tested on cell samples and then on animals. Next, the Food and Drug Administration reviews the results of such tests. If the treatment appears to be promising, permission for a clinical trial is granted.

A clinical trial is divided into three phases. Phase I is a beginning trial. Its primary objective is to establish whether or not the treatment is safe for humans. Once the safety is established, phase II treatments focus on determining the effectiveness of the treatment. In ovarian cancer trials this is done by measuring CA-125 levels, survival rates, and tumor growth. Phase III trials compare the treatment's effectiveness to proven treatments.

In all three phases, participants are given some form of treatment. In phase I and II, all patients are administered the test treatment. In phase III, a control group is administered a proven treatment, while other subjects are administered the test treatment. No one receives a placebo, which is a substance that looks like the treatment being tested but actually has no medicinal value.

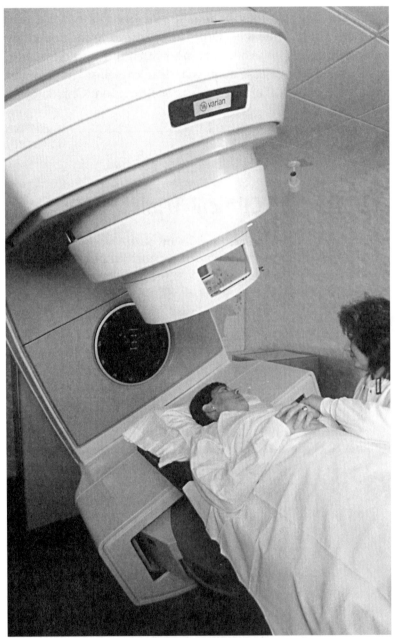

As part of an ovarian cancer patient's radiation treatment, a particle accelerator is used to help slow down the growth of abnormal cells in her body.

did I finally say to someone, 'What is recurrence?' I found out that the chances were great that the cancer would come back. That was discouraging at first. Now I know that the possibility is there but I choose not to let that weigh me down."[34]

Most initial recurrences of ovarian cancer occur within five years of primary treatment. There is no guarantee that an initial recurrence will not occur at a later date, but it is far less likely. Just as before, when cancer recurs, surgery is performed, the patient is debulked, and chemotherapy is administered. Often a different combination of drugs is used in an effort to thwart resistant cancer cells. However, the recurrence of ovarian cancer indicates that the cancer is both aggressive and somewhat resistant to medication. This means that once ovarian cancer recurs, it is likely to recur again. Therefore, the goal of treatment is not so much to cure the disease but to extend the period of remission.

Once chemotherapy for a recurrence is complete, most individuals once again go into remission. A second remission may be lengthy, lasting three or more years, or it may last a few months. Generally, whenever ovarian cancer recurs, chemotherapy is administered. Sometimes radiation is also administered. However, because radiation treatment for ovarian cancer is directed at the abdomen and can damage the patient's kidneys and bowels, it is not used frequently. Some patients join clinical trials, where new experimental drugs are used. Indeed, many women live with ovarian cancer for years, controlling their ovarian cancer in the same manner as people control other chronic diseases such as diabetes or heart disease. Cancer specialists Jimmie C. Holland and Sheldon Lewis explain:

> Many tumors today recur or progress after their primary treatment only to be successfully controlled for years by . . . chemotherapy or surgery. The dictum that recurrent cancer is death is surely no longer true. Many cancers can be treated on a long-term basis so they become chronic conditions. A cure may not be possible with today's knowledge, but effective control of the tumor, often for years, has changed the outlook.[35]

Side Effects of Treatment

Any time ovarian cancer treatment is administered, it can cause distressing side effects and health risks. Because it introduces toxic chemicals that kill not just cancer cells but healthy, normal cells, chemotherapy takes a toll on the body. Some patients experience persistent pain during chemotherapy as normal cells are destroyed, while others do not. Each individual reacts differently to chemotherapy. Some people encounter frequent and severe side effects, while other patients are hardly bothered by chemotherapy. But the most common side effects of chemotherapy include fatigue, hair loss, nausea and vomiting, poor appetite, and a decrease in white and red blood cell levels.

Digestive Problems

Because normal cells in an individual's digestive tract are especially vulnerable to chemotherapy, most people experience nausea and vomiting on the day of chemotherapy and for two or three days thereafter. Patients are given antinausea medication to help control this problem. However, antinausea medicine often causes constipation. Brown explains:

> You will most likely have some nausea and queasiness; I describe it as like the feeling one would have after eating half a cheesecake. The treatments use pretty powerful medicines, and it takes the body some time to process them. So there are two kinds of side effects: the immediate effects of digestive problems caused by the chemo and anti-nausea drug effects on the digestive tract, which will resolve themselves quickly.[36]

Feelings of nausea also lessen an individual's appetite, as does chemotherapy medication. Chemotherapy can also affect a person's sense of taste and can cause patients to have an unpleasant metallic taste in their mouths. Steroids, too, can dull a person's sense of taste. Radner explained:

> Eating was very unpleasant. I craved salty things because I could taste them. I ate what I ordinarily wouldn't eat. I wanted cheeseburgers, cheese and pickles. Lettuce and vegetables

tasted like plastic. The highly salty, tasty things were good, but bland food tasted like something they weren't and that was too strange. It was too weird when a carrot tasted like a ceramic kitchen magnet.[37]

Hair Loss

Follicles in which hairs grow are also vulnerable to chemotherapy. When the cells in hair follicles are destroyed, hair growing in the follicles falls out. Chemotherapy patients usually lose most of their body hair, including that on their head, as well as their eyebrows and eyelashes. This is temporary and once chemotherapy is over, the hair grows back. Radner recalled: "I woke up and the first thing my eyes focused on was hairs all over my pillowcase. I reached into my punk haircut and a bunch of strands came out in my hand. Looking down onto the bathtub floor while I was shampooing, I saw it was covered with hair swirling in the drain—my hair."[38]

Although ovarian cancer patients often lose their hair and muscle tone during chemotherapy, their hair grows back and they regain strength after the treatment.

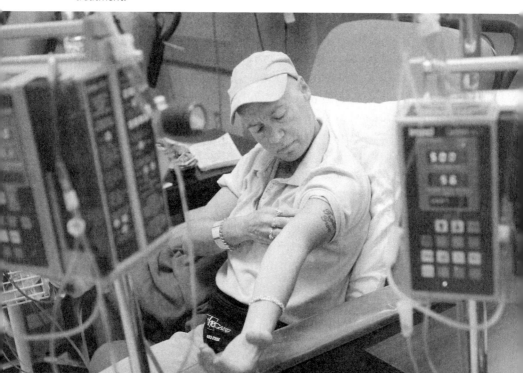

Lower Red and White Blood Cell Counts

Because red and white blood cells tend to reproduce quickly, they, too, are susceptible to chemotherapy. Therefore, many individuals undergoing chemotherapy experience a temporary decrease in red and white blood cells, which return to normal once chemotherapy is finished.

Since the job of white blood cells is to fight infection, people are more vulnerable to contagious diseases when white blood cell counts are lowered. Lower red blood cell counts can also cause problems. Red blood cells carry oxygen-laden hemoglobin, which the body needs for strength and energy. Consequently, when red blood cell counts fall, patients are easily fatigued. Anita recalls: "Throughout chemo, my mother was very tired. She never complained. She would just lie down and sleep a lot."[39]

Complementing Conventional Treatment with Alternative Treatment

To better cope with the side effects of chemotherapy, many women with ovarian cancer combine traditional medical treatment with alternative treatments. This is known as complementary treatment.

Alternative treatments have not undergone strict testing to prove their safety and effectiveness, as conventional treatments have. The job of the Food and Drug Administration (FDA) is to confirm that the advantages of a treatment outweigh any possible health risks, and to regulate and set standards for approved treatments. It does not approve most alternative treatments.

Most experts agree that alternative treatments cannot replace surgery and chemotherapy in controlling ovarian cancer. When alternative treatments are used without traditional treatment, their effectiveness is speculative at best. Ovarian cancer expert Vivian Von Gruenigen, speaking at the 2004 meeting of the Gynecologic Cancer Foundation, explained: "The research is very limited, and the question is what does it do to the woman's overall body? What does it do to the tumor? And the data that we have right now is that there is no CAM [complementary/alternative medicine] that enhance cure."[40]

Visualization

Visualization is a popular complementary cancer treatment. Like meditation, visualization uses the mind to calm the body and promote healing. While practicing visualization, individuals envision a particular goal. For example, many individuals visualize chemotherapy medications going directly to tumor sites and destroying cancer cells. Then they visualize their body healing. In addition, many patients use visualization to help them minimize the side effects of chemotherapy by visualizing themselves free of nausea and fatigue.

Individuals use a variety of images when practicing visualization. Some model their visualization after video games. These people imagine figures, like those in Pac-Man, marauding through their body and gobbling up cancer cells. Others envision miniature armies, or a healing light moving through their bodies. What each person visualizes is different. Gilda Radner used the image of a towel in her visualizations. She explained: "The towel was fresh from the dryer, warm and pink. In my mind I would pick through all the little strands of terry cloth to make sure there weren't any black dots of cancer. If I saw any, I would pick them out, the way you'd remove lint from a towel."

There is no conclusive proof that visualization works. But according to the American Cancer Society, forty-six studies conducted between 1966 and 1998 found visualization effective in controlling stress and anxiety, and in relieving the side effects of chemotherapy.

Even so, many ovarian cancer patients and health care professionals say that combining certain alternative treatments with surgery and chemotherapy can be beneficial. In fact, an estimated 50 percent of the fifty-six National Cancer Institute cancer centers in the United States offer some form of alternative treatment. National Cancer Institute director Andrew C. von Eschenbach explains:

M.D. Anderson Cancer Center, for example, where I was a surgeon for many years, has a Place of Wellness that helps patients with issues around nutrition, introduces them to meditation, relaxation, exercises, yoga. You're seeing efforts to complement the tried-and-true interventions with additional ones that may be helpful.[41]

Common Complementary Treatments

There are a number of alternative treatments, such as meditation and diet, that ovarian cancer patients can combine with conventional treatment. Meditation is used to enhance the effectiveness of chemotherapy and to reduce negative side effects. Meditation is a process in which an individual recites or chants a word or phrase in order to calm her mind and, thus, relax and reduce stress. This is especially important for those individuals who are fearful of chemotherapy. Fear causes a stress reaction in the body and, since stress interferes with the healing process, it can actually worsen a person's health. Reducing fear, anxiety, and stress helps strengthen an individual's ability to heal. In addition, because meditation can produce feelings of peace and well-being, it reduces frequent mood swings that often accompany steroid use. Brown explains how meditation helped her:

> I was totally overwhelmed and frightened, by the shock of surgery, the specter of chemotherapy, the fear of death. . . . I learned to meditate to acknowledge and dissolve my fear. . . . One might see meditation as giving a sense of control, and it did provide that. But it also imparted peace and, in peace, there's more room for healing than in fear.[42]

Diet

Some ovarian cancer patients change their diet as part of their treatment regime. They try to improve their diet by increasing their intake of foods that supposedly contain cancer-fighting properties, including fruits and vegetables that contain antioxidants. Antioxidants are substances that prevent oxidation, a process in which cells are weakened when they come in contact with oxygen molecules. Weakened cells may be more likely to mutate.

There have been a number of studies looking into the role diet plays in fighting cancer. Although there is no evidence that eating a diet rich in fruits and vegetables can cure cancer, it can certainly improve general health. Scientists theorize that this may reduce an individual's risk of developing cancer. It can also help counter constipation and improve digestive problems that accompany chemotherapy, which improves a patient's quality of life.

It is clear that treatment for ovarian cancer can be difficult, with many unpleasant side effects. Complementary treatment often helps ovarian cancer patients cope with these side effects and, thus, enhance their quality of life. Such treatments, however, cannot cure ovarian cancer. Surgery and chemotherapy can. And when ovarian cancer is aggressive and a cure is not likely, surgery and chemotherapy can control the disease and extend a patient's life.

Chapter 4

Living with Ovarian Cancer

L IVING WITH OVARIAN cancer is challenging. Patients must cope with the toll cancer takes on their bodies, the side effects of treatment, and the emotional issues caused by the threat of recurrence. But when women with ovarian cancer take steps to cope with these challenges, they gain control over their lives, which, in turn, improves the quality of their lives.

Coping with Fatigue

Both ovarian cancer and chemotherapy can cause fatigue. Although ovarian cancer patients try to maintain their normal lives, many report that overwhelming tiredness makes it difficult to perform everyday tasks. Maintaining a balance between action and rest helps women with ovarian cancer to cope. Brown advises, "At some point, you may hit the wall of fatigue, and there's nothing to do but stop and rest."[43]

Consequently, many ovarian cancer patients take frequent naps. Besides helping to conserve energy, napping also promotes healing. A 2004 study conducted at Stanford University School of Medicine in Palo Alto, California, found that getting adequate sleep helps women with many types of cancer, including ovarian cancer, fight the disease. Researchers theorize that in addition to strengthening the body and, thus, building the body's defenses, sleep stimulates the production of a chemical called melatonin, which inhibits the ovaries' production of estrogen. Excess estrogen production, scientists believe, may stimulate ovarian cell division, which can lead to the growth of cancerous cells.

Short naps while at work can help women with ovarian cancer cope with the tremendous fatigue that is a typical side effect of chemotherapy.

In addition to napping, many women with ovarian cancer make changes in their regular routines in order to conserve energy. They often cut back on regular activities. Such cutbacks include reducing work hours or taking a leave of absence from work, curtailing social activities, and getting help with such tasks as child care, housecleaning, shopping, and cooking from family, friends, or professionals. Kimberly, an ovarian cancer survivor explains:

> We . . . hired a full-time nanny. This was money well spent as it gave me time to rest while keeping the children busy and cared for. . . . I just didn't have the energy or stamina for Play-Dough, tea parties, and tag, or meals, laundry, and baths. My husband also increased the frequency of our housecleaning service. Having the children and house cared for allowed me to focus all my energy on healing.[44]

When fatigue is a result of a low red blood cell count, many patients take medication that helps to rebuild red blood cells lost during chemotherapy. The medication is identical to erythropoietin, a substance that is produced by the body to stimulate red blood cell production. Since having more red blood cells increases strength and energy, stimulating the production of red blood cells in this manner helps many individuals cope with fatigue.

Avoiding Infection

Another challenge women with ovarian cancer face is the risk of infection. When chemotherapy lowers an ovarian cancer patient's white blood cell count, she becomes more susceptible to contracting an infection. Therefore, in order to keep themselves healthy, women with ovarian cancer take steps to minimize the risk of infection when their white blood cell count is low. This involves avoiding people who have been sick and avoiding enclosed, crowded areas in which germs can easily spread. Therefore, patients avoid visits to crowded malls or movie theaters and rides on crowded buses, subways, or airplanes. Ovarian cancer patients also find that washing their hands frequently

Even routine dental work exposes ovarian cancer patients to the threat of infection from minor cuts or abrasions caused by the dentist's instruments.

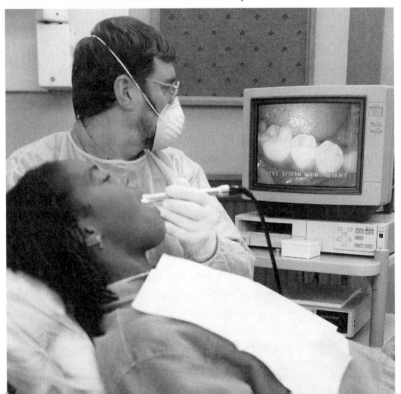

helps them to remove any germs they may have come in contact with, helping prevent infection.

In an effort to prevent infection, many women with ovarian cancer avoid dental checkups while they are receiving chemotherapy. Even the small cuts and scrapes that may occur in a patient's mouth and gums when teeth are cleaned can turn into serious infections for people with low white blood cell counts. For the same reason, many ovarian cancer patients switch to a soft toothbrush, which is less likely to damage their gums. They also wear gloves while gardening and doing housework in an effort to avoid cuts and scrapes.

Coping with Nausea

Nausea and vomiting caused by chemotherapy present another challenge. Besides taking antinausea drugs, some women with ovarian cancer drink herbal teas made from ginger or mint. These both have antinausea properties and have been used as digestive aids for thousands of years. In some cases, patients find they can lower their dosage of antinausea medication when they use these herbs. Brown explains: "On one course [of chemotherapy] using a milder drug, I got by with drinking peppermint tea and candied ginger. Chinese sailors use ginger to offset seasickness, and it worked during my treatment."[45]

Many women with ovarian cancer find that drinking at least a gallon of water or other fluids such as juice or Gatorade each day for two days before going into chemotherapy helps reduce nausea. Being well hydrated helps flush excess chemotherapy medication, which would otherwise linger in the body, causing nausea and vomiting, out of the digestive tract.

Drinking plenty of fluids also combats constipation, a side effect of antinausea drugs. Fluids help soften feces and prevent them from becoming sticky, thus reducing constipation. In addition, being well hydrated helps reduce fatigue, which is a symptom of dehydration. Drinking adequate fluids is so important in helping women with ovarian cancer meet the challenge of daily living that Evelyn Larrison, a nurse and gynecologic oncology consultant, advises: "I suggest that patients get ten magnets and place them on the front of their refrigerator. Then, every time they drink a glass of fluid, they should remove the magnet to the side of the refrigerator. This is a great visual reminder to drink a lot of fluids."[46]

Coping with Poor Appetite and Weight Loss

Nausea, combined with the effects of cancer and the tendency of chemotherapy medications to affect the taste buds, leads many individuals with ovarian cancer to experience poor appetite and excess weight loss. Poor appetite is a problem because even though women with ovarian cancer may not feel well enough to eat, it is important that they get adequate nutrition in order to strengthen their bodies, maximize their energy, and maintain wellness. In fact, doctors estimate that people being treated for cancer need about 20 percent more nutrients than healthy individuals. This is because both chemotherapy and cancer deplete the body of valuable nutrients.

Getting adequate nutrition also enhances the effects of chemotherapy medication. Research indicates that well-nourished people are better able to absorb and tolerate the effects of chemotherapy drugs than are those who are poorly nourished.

Ovarian cancer patients meet the challenge posed by poor appetite in a number of ways. Some eat frequent small, light meals. Many individuals say that this type of eating pattern is easier to tolerate than three large, heavy meals a day. Brown explains: "As important as it is to eat, it is hard to say 'eat lightly' when you might not feel like eating at all, but right after treatment when your body is trying to process chemo, I found it helpful to eat light, nutritious foods that I could easily digest. It also helps to eat small quantities all day rather than a few large meals."[47]

Indeed, in an effort to eat more often, many patients carry nutritious snacks with them at all times so that when they do feel hungry, they have food handy. Some patients substitute a favorite dish for a more standard meal. Anita recalls: "My mother ate very small portions. Certain things didn't taste right to her. With chemo you really lose your taste buds. But she liked fresh

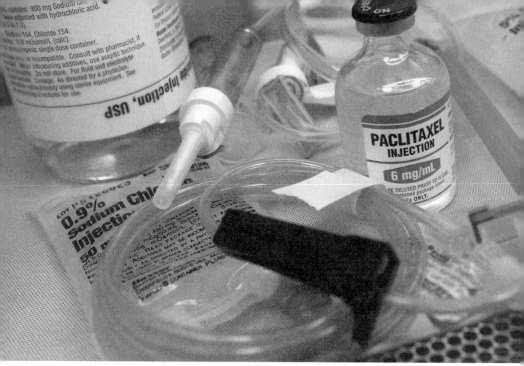

Studies have shown that chemotherapy medications such as these are tolerated and absorbed better by patients who eat a healthy diet.

fruit. She would eat fresh fruit, and vanilla ice cream with peaches. That had always been her favorite food."[48]

Substituting liquid nourishment for solid food is another way women with ovarian cancer cope with appetite problems, while those able to tolerate light meals often add nutrient-rich liquids to their diet in order to battle weight loss. For the same reason, many ovarian cancer patients add calorie-rich foods such as ice cream, whole milk, cream, or yogurt to such drinks.

Liquid food supplements include commercially sold nutrient-rich drinks as well as homemade shakes, egg nogs, and smoothies prepared with protein powder. Protein is needed to maintain and repair body tissues. When cancer is present, getting adequate protein is especially important for repairing damage to the body. This may be in the form of meat, for those who are able to tolerate solid food, or in protein-rich beverages. Anita recalls: "My dad made my mother protein shakes or smoothies with fresh fruit, different fruit juices, protein powder, and vanilla ice cream. He'd do anything to get the protein she needed in her."[49]

Getting moderate exercise also helps women with ovarian cancer cope. Exercise increases the appetite and, because exercise

Cancer and Exercise

Exercising has become an important way individuals cope with cancer. An Associated Press report in the *Las Cruces Sun News* describes a growing trend in living with cancer:

> More than 150 cancer patients a year trudge into Julie Main's weight room, often pale and weak next to the more buff regulars at her California gym. For 10 weeks, in a free program backed by the local cancer hospital, they rebuild muscles their disease has laid to waste.

> It's part of a slowly growing trend, special exercise programs for patients in the midst of grueling chemotherapy and even those with very advanced cancer, people once told to take it easy.

> New nutrition and fitness guidelines for the 9.5 million Americans living after a cancer diagnosis say those programs are right on track; appropriate exercise can help even the weakest eat better, feel less fatigue, and recover faster.

This breast cancer survivor works out to regain her strength following surgery to remove her lymph glands.

builds muscle, it also helps ovarian cancer patients meet the challenge of excess weight loss.

Exercise also decreases feelings of fatigue, strengthens muscles and joints, and promotes a feeling of well-being. Research shows that regular exercise may also reduce an individual's risk of developing cancer. Although ovarian cancer patients may not feel able to participate in vigorous exercise, even exercising for five-minute intervals three times a day helps strengthen the patient and increase her appetite. Walking, swimming, yoga, tai chi, and bicycling are all forms of exercise recommended by the National Ovarian Cancer Association.

Coping with Pain

Exercise also helps ovarian cancer patients cope with another challenge: pain. Tenderness and soreness are common after surgery. Chemotherapy can cause persistent pain in some individuals. Tumors that have not been removed can press on nerves, bones, and organs, causing pain and pressure. Exercise stimulates production of endorphins, natural chemicals that give exercisers a feeling of well-being and reduce feelings of pain.

Practicing meditation also helps many patients deal with pain. So does pain medication, which is often administered to help women with ovarian cancer cope. Such medication may be given in pill form, or a patch may be applied that delivers the medication through the skin. Often patients are treated by a health care professional who specializes in pain management. They help regulate the patient's pain medication dosage in order to accurately control the pain.

Participating in enjoyable activities that distract patients from painful sensations is another way individuals deal with pain. Activities such as visiting with friends and family, watching a favorite television show, painting, quilting, and listening to soothing music are all things women with ovarian cancer say help to take their mind off pain. Brown explains: "Watching an engrossing drama or comedy and working with my hands (I've learned to knit, crochet, and sculpt in clay) help to alleviate pain by distracting my attention elsewhere."[50]

Coping with Hair Loss

Coping with hair loss is another challenge women with ovarian cancer face. Hair loss due to cancer treatment can be disheartening, and many people report that it lowers their self-confidence and inhibits their social interactions. This is because hair loss, on women especially, visibly marks an individual as a cancer patient, different from healthy individuals. It becomes a reminder of illness for the patient herself as well as for others. Indeed, many patients say that hair loss impacts the way others treat them. A 2002 survey of 267 women diagnosed with cancer conducted by the Look Good . . . Feel Better program, a support organization that helps cancer patients cope with hair loss and other changes in their appearance, looked at this issue. The survey found that among the women who experienced significant treatment-related changes in their appearance, 72 percent noticed that others treated them differently. Radner remembered:

> The most difficult part of the whole chemotherapy for me was losing my hair. . . . I couldn't stop crying, couldn't stop feeling ugly. . . . I didn't want to go out of the house; I didn't want to go to any dinners or any parties. . . . It seemed so unfair, not only to have to go through chemotherapy, but to feel marked with baldness like the mark on a house that was quarantined when someone had scarlet fever in the old days.[51]

Many women find that getting a short haircut before they begin chemotherapy helps make the transition easier. According to hair care experts at the Look Good . . . Feel Better program, when hair starts to thin, short hair tends to look fuller than long hair. Once hair loss occurs, women with ovarian cancer wear wigs, hairpieces, hats, scarves, and turbans until chemotherapy ends and their hair grows back. Radner explained: "I bought a whole bunch of scarves. . . . I wore the caps Grace [her friend] had made me and wrapped the long, narrow . . . scarves around them. The happier I was, the more I piled on my head. I dressed like a harem girl. . . . I had a whole look. . . . I was even in style."[52]

Organizations such as the American Cancer Society and Cancer Care help women in need pay for a wig. Other organizations, such

A cosmetologist gives makeup tips to a cancer patient who has lost her eyebrows and eyelashes as a result of chemotherapy.

as Look Good . . . Feel Better, conduct group and one-on-one sessions in hospitals and cancer centers throughout the United States with professional beauticians and cosmetologists. These sessions instruct cancer patients on how to style wigs and wrap scarves and turbans, as well as providing makeup tips for problems such as loss of eyelashes and eyebrows, among other things. Indeed, 86 percent of women surveyed by the organization attribute looking better to feeling better. Kathleen attended one such makeup session. She recalls:

> It was incredible. I was starting to lose my eyelashes and my eyebrows so I needed the makeup tips to make it appear that I had them. Look Good . . . Feel Better was a wonderful class. . . . Throughout my experience with cancer—I had to give blood, I had to give my veins. I had to give myself. Look Good . . . Feel Better was giving back to me and it's great.[53]

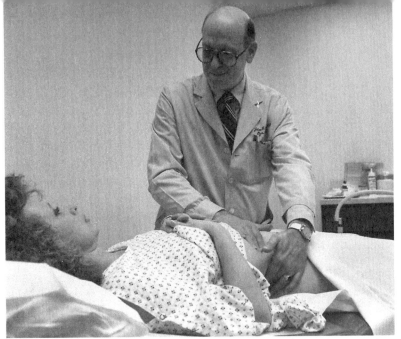

Patients whose ovarian cancer has gone into remission must undergo regular monitoring by cancer specialists to detect any recurrence of the disease.

Medical Monitoring

When chemotherapy is over and the unpleasant side effects have disappeared, ovarian cancer survivors still must undergo careful monitoring in order to determine if the disease has recurred. This involves frequent doctor visits. Usually these are scheduled every two to four months for the first two years. After that, doctor visits are spaced further apart, usually every six months for the next three years, and yearly thereafter. A CA-125 test is administered during every doctor visit, as is a complete physical and pelvic exam. A chest X-ray, mammogram, and imaging tests of the patient's abdomen and pelvis are administered at least once a year.

Such monitoring helps confirm that the patient is healthy. Because of the frequency of medical monitoring, a recurrence of ovarian cancer is likely to be discovered in an early, more controllable stage. Consequently, frequent medical monitoring can extend an individual's life.

Coping with Emotional Issues

Fighting ovarian cancer presents emotional challenges. Undergoing chemotherapy and coping with its side effects is stressful. Medical monitoring is another source of anxiety. Each doctor visit brings with it uncertainty. Knowing that ovarian cancer can recur at any time, and that a recurrence could be fatal, takes an emotional toll on patients, and some suffer from depression. Linda, an ovarian cancer survivor, explains: "Your life is on a roller coaster. You just don't know what to plan for. I mean, it is downright terrifying. You ask yourself, Where can I go? What's going to happen to my family, my relationships, my work? Your family and friends really don't know what to say. It's just an unimaginably traumatic turn in your life journey."[54]

Dealing with emotional issues allows individuals to gain control over their lives. Seeing a health care professional is one way ovarian cancer patients deal with emotional problems. Besides providing patients with emotional support, a psychiatrist can prescribe antidepressant and antianxiety medications. By producing a feeling of well-being, such medications help relieve symptoms of anxiety and depression. This improves the patient's quality of life. According to Massachusetts oncologist Michael Van Seiden,

> Ovarian cancer can cause great distress. Women often experience loss of sleep, fatigue, and a loss of enjoyment and interest in activities they once loved. It's just very, very stressful. . . . Patients say, "Of course I am depressed," assuming that this is just part of the cancer experience and that nothing can be done about it. Medications . . . can allow you to function fully, get things done in your day, and feel good about your life.[55]

Talking to a mental health professional about emotional issues is another way women with ovarian cancer face emotional challenges. Often individuals are reluctant to burden their loved ones with their fears and anxieties. Talking with a mental health professional provides individuals with an outlet to express their concerns.

In *The Human Side of Cancer*, authors Jimmie C. Holland and Sheldon Lewis interview cancer patients who describe how seeing a mental health professional benefited them: "The therapist is like a sounding board," one patient explains. Another adds: "I have someone with whom I can express my worst fears without burdening my family with them." A third says, "I no longer feel so isolated now, so I can share how I feel with someone else."[56]

Getting Help from a Support Group

Participating in a support group is another way ovarian cancer patients can express their feelings. Cancer support groups are made up of cancer patients and survivors who share their experiences. There are support groups specifically for women with ovarian cancer, as well as mixed groups for people with any type of cancer. In a group setting, individuals share their feelings and exchange information and advice about fighting and living with cancer.

Support groups also give newly diagnosed patients an opportunity to meet ovarian cancer survivors. Such meetings give many women hope that they too will survive. Sara, an ovarian cancer survivor, explains:

> I started going to the weekly support group after my first chemotherapy treatment and it was just so helpful. People asked me questions and shared their experiences, which helped me know what to expect and prepared me for things I was about to go through.
>
> I think that being with other cancer patients is one of the most practical sources of help you can find. You learn so much from the experiences of people who have gone before you.

For many people diagnosed with cancer, local support groups of cancer survivors become a valuable source of hope, strength, and faith.

The Wellness Community

Gilda Radner participated in the Wellness Community, a national organization that offers support and educational workshops for cancer patients and their loved ones. In *It's Always Something*, she described her first visit:

> It was a cute little yellow house with a plaque on the front that said, "The Wellness Community." We [Radner and a friend] walked into what looked like a living room in anybody's home. There were two women there with pink sweatshirts on that said "The Wellness Community" and big buttons that said "VICTOR" on them. There was a sweet woman named Joyce who gave us flyers and information and made us comfortable. There were three couches and a rug on the floor and phones ringing in other rooms. . . .
>
> About ten after eleven the room was pretty much filled with maybe forty people. The two group leaders, Flo and Beth, both eleven-year survivors of cancer told their stories of cancer. They explained what The Wellness Community was and what it had to offer every person there. Amazingly, everything was free. There were group therapy sessions that met for two hours a week, available at many different times during the week called "participant groups." These groups were the only Wellness Community activities that required a commitment. They were facilitated by licensed therapists. Everything else was on a drop-in basis, including instruction in guided imagery and visualization and relaxation three nights a week. There were group sessions for spouses or family members of cancer patients, nutrition and cooking discussions, lectures by doctors—oncologists and psychiatrists—workshops on anger management, potluck dinners and parties, therapy through painting, vocalizing, improvising—all techniques that would help in stress management and improve the quality of someone's life.

Actor Gene Wilder founded Gilda's Club in New York City to honor the memory of his wife, Gilda Radner. The club offers a variety of services to ovarian cancer patients.

You see how they handled it, how they walked the road. Of course, some make decisions similar to the ones you would make and some don't, but it's just so useful to have them as an example.

On the emotional side, watching people who were farther down the road than me was just so awesome, inspiring, and encouraging. Such a group really is a community—and community is very important during such a difficult time.[57]

Support groups can be found everywhere. Most hospitals sponsor support groups, as do many community organizations and religious institutions. There are even Internet support groups for individuals who are unable to leave their homes. "My daily support group is the online Ovarian Problems Discussion List hosted by ACOR [American Cancer Online Resources]," ovarian cancer survivor Chris explains:

> It is such a useful resource. There have been many times that I was facing new treatment and wrote to the list to ask women, "What do you know about this drug?" We all help each other with questions and keep each other informed about what is out there. I've corresponded with women as far away as England, China, and South America! Even online, you can get very close with other women.[58]

The Wellness Community and Gilda's Club are other options. Both organizations have locations throughout the United States. They offer professionally led support groups and educational programs for cancer patients and their families in a comfortable environment. Harold Benjamin, the founder of the Wellness Community and the husband of a cancer survivor, describes the Wellness Community in this way:

> It is a place to learn to participate in your fight for recovery along with your physician. We feel that if you participate in your fight for recovery, you will enhance the quality of your life and just may enhance the possibility of your recovery. Your first line of defense against cancer is your immune system. Scientific studies have shown that depression weakens the immune system—we are here to teach you the tools for the pursuit of happiness.[59]

Indeed, participating in a support group is just one of the many steps women with ovarian cancer take in order to make their lives happier. Although living with ovarian cancer is challenging, women who fight to meet these challenges feel happier and more in control of their lives. Radner maintained: "What I've learned the hard way is there is always something you can do. It may not be the easy thing to do. . . . But there is always something you can do."[60]

Chapter 5

What the Future Holds

O varian cancer research is focused on developing a simple and reliable diagnostic test, as well as more effective treatments. Currently, the lack of an effective diagnostic test for ovarian cancer means the majority of women with the disease are not diagnosed until their cancer is advanced. This makes curing the disease difficult and worsens the patient's prognosis. Therefore, scientists are working hard to develop a reliable diagnostic test for ovarian cancer. Kathryn Zoon, director of the FDA's Center for Biologics Evaluation and Research, explains, "Simple, accurate, and non-invasive methods for the early detection of epithelial ovarian cancer may improve the quality of life and survival and reduce unnecessary suffering for patients."[61]

At the same time, scientists are developing safer, more effective treatments that could cure ovarian cancer or prolong remission periods. Better treatment therapies and more effective diagnostic tests should extend the lives of women with ovarian cancer considerably.

A Diagnostic Blood Test

In a joint effort, scientists at the National Cancer Institute, the FDA, and a number of private companies are working on developing a simple blood test that accurately diagnoses ovarian cancer. The test uses a promising approach to analyzing blood samples called proteomics, which is the study of proteins in cells, tissues, and blood.

Proteins, which are found in every tissue in the body, direct the actions of cells. Scientists have found that all cells shed protein into the bloodstream, but healthy cells and cancerous cells shed different combinations and quantities of protein that form different patterns in the bloodstream. Protein patterns also differ among different kinds of tumors. The protein pattern of breast cancer, for example, is different than that of ovarian cancer. Thus, each type of cancer has its own protein pattern or fingerprint.

Scientists do not know why different tumors have different fingerprints. But they are using this knowledge to develop a blood test that uses high-tech equipment to detect a specific protein pattern associated with ovarian cancer.

In the test, blood samples are placed in a machine called a spectroscope, which is attached to a computer. The spectroscope emits waves of infrared radiation that protein molecules in the blood absorb and convert to heat. Different protein molecules absorb different amounts of radiation and, therefore, produce different quantities of heat.

Scientists are optimistic that the survival rate of ovarian cancer patients can be increased by early detection using new technology like the spectroscope.

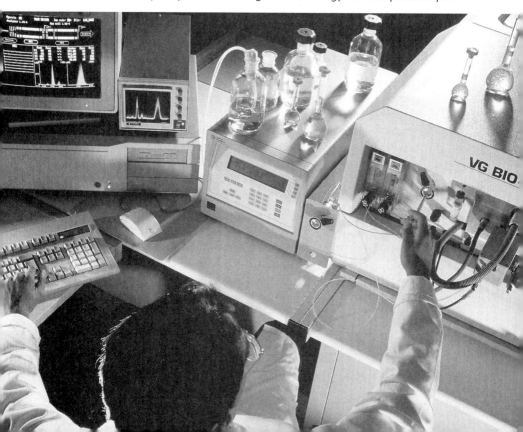

National Cancer Institute Announces Cancer Goal

In 2003 Andrew C. von Eschenbach, director of the National Cancer Institute, announced the institute's newest goal—to end "death and suffering from cancer by 2015." In an interview with *AARP Bulletin* author Claudia Dreifus, von Eschenbach explains this goal:

> I did not say we are going to eliminate cancer. I don't know when that will happen, if ever. We are asking, "What can we reasonably expect?" And the answer is that there's much more we can do to eliminate the burden of the disease on those who get it.

> Beyond that, I see a time coming when we'll be able to develop interventions that not only prevent and eliminate the disease in some people, but that also control cancer in others—much like we control high blood pressure and diabetes today. So thanks to research there'll be people who will live with it and who will not die from cancer. There'll be others who won't get it in the first place.

> We used to think of cancer as something that just happened to a person. Now we understand cancer as a long process. It may start with a genetic predisposition or because of things you were exposed to. The process continues to the point where it becomes a tumor that spreads and can take your life. But it is not something that happens instantaneously.

> By understanding cancer at the genetic, molecular and cellular levels, we can intervene much more effectively than ever before to pre-empt the cancer process. Treatment in the future will be by design, based on your genes, what chemicals they are expressing, what the specific tumor looks like, how it works, where it is.

The heat waves bounce back from the blood sample to the computer, where software translates the heat waves into a graph, or pattern, that appears on the computer monitor.

In order to identify an ovarian cancer pattern, scientists first used the spectroscope to compare blood samples of healthy women with those of women with ovarian cancer. Once the characteristics of ovarian cancer were established, scientists analyzed blood samples of sixty-six healthy women and fifty women with ovarian cancer. The researchers correctly identified all the blood samples of women with ovarian cancer, including a number of stage I cases. They correctly identified sixty-three of the healthy blood samples, misdiagnosing three healthy samples as cancerous.

National Cancer Institute researchers are currently conducting similar tests on larger groups in an effort to verify the accuracy of proteomics tests. So far, the results have been encouraging, especially since the test appears to accurately diagnose early stage ovarian cancer. Indeed, researchers and physicians throughout the United States are hopeful. Beth Y. Karlan, the director of gynecologic oncology at Cedars-Sinai Medical Center in Los Angeles, California, asserts: "I am optimistic that within five years there will be a truly reliable screening test. Such a test would improve survival from ovarian cancer more than any new therapies."[62]

Ovarian Pap Test

Currently the only way to diagnose ovarian cancer is through surgery. Scientists at Northwestern University in Chicago, Illinois, are working on a different diagnostic test. This test is similar to a Pap test, in which cells taken from a woman's cervix are examined for evidence of cervical cancer. However, because of the location of the ovaries, a small incision must be made in the patient's abdomen for the new ovarian cancer test to be administered. Therefore, the ovarian Pap test is more appropriate for high-risk women than it is for the general population.

The test, which can be administered in a doctor's office, utilizes a laparoscope, a lighted, tubular instrument with a camera-like device and a scooplike tool on the tip. The laparoscope is placed inside the incision, where it takes pictures of the patient's ovaries and gathers cell samples. The pictures can be seen immediately on a computer monitor, while the cells are analyzed in a laboratory.

The ovarian Pap test is currently being tested in an ongoing clinical trial known as the National Ovarian Cancer Early Detection Program and Genetic Study at Northwestern University and other locations. In a five-year period, the ovarian Pap test will be used as a diagnostic tool on six thousand women, five thousand of whom are at high risk of developing ovarian cancer, and one thousand of whom have the disease.

In addition to testing the ovarian Pap test's reliability, researchers plan to gather ovarian epithelial cells from at-risk women, as well as from women in different stages of ovarian cancer. The cells will then be compared. Researchers think that by studying the cells, they will be able to develop a profile of changes in ovarian cells as cancer develops and advances. If this can be accomplished, then scientists hope to use another new tool, molecular imaging, in diagnosing ovarian cancer.

Molecular Imaging

Molecular imaging is a new form of imaging that produces images of targeted cells and the molecules that make up the cells. If scientists can develop a molecular profile of ovarian cancer cells at different stages of development, they can use molecular imaging to determine whether ovarian cancer is developing, or present. The stage can be established in the same manner. Neurobiologist Jeff Lichtman of Washington University's Molecular Imaging Center in St. Louis, Missouri, explains: "It's really an exciting time. These are phenomena that were never seen before because we didn't have the tools to see them."[63]

In addition, molecular imaging can be used to determine the effects of different drugs on cancer cells. For example, scientists theorize that some, but not all, patients develop a protein within cancer cells that makes the cells resistant to certain chemotherapy medications. These patients often go through six complete cycles of chemotherapy before learning that their cancer is unresponsive to treatment. Molecular imaging will help scientists examine cancer cells for the presence of the suspicious protein before chemotherapy starts. David Piwnica-Worms, director of the Molecular Imaging Center, states: "The ultimate goal would be to use these types of noninvasive imaging tools up front at diagnosis. If a patient looks like they're multi-drug resistant, we may want to . . . consider other forms of therapy."[64]

Target Drugs

By using proteomics to analyze chemicals and proteins that cancer cells secrete as they grow and molecular imaging to view changes in cancer cells, scientists hope to identify a tumor's weak point. Scientists theorize that tumors have different weak points based on their location and structure. Once a tumor's weak point is established, a treatment strategy can be devised using new drugs that hone in on that part of the tumor. These drugs are designed to attack a tumor's weak point without affecting the rest of the body. Tamar Peretz of Hadassah Hospital in Jerusalem, Israel, explains: "We're working toward new ways of evaluating tumors, molecularly and pathologically [through blood analysis]. Ultimately, I believe we'll be able to identify specific markers on each tumor and define treatment for each individual patient according to the tumor."[65]

For example, scientists already have learned that many stomach and blood cancer tumors produce abnormal amounts of enzymes or proteins called tyrosine kinases, which facilitate the division and spread of cancer cells. A new drug called Gleevec inhibits the production of tyrosine kinases. Tests in Basel, Switzerland, have shown that treatment with Gleevec stops leukemia (a type of blood cancer) and stomach cancer cells from dividing.

A number of studies are being conducted to see if ovarian cancer cells also produce this or other damaging proteins that can be targeted in treatment. In fact, researchers at the Fox Chase Cancer Center in Philadelphia, Pennsylvania, and at M.D. Anderson Cancer Center in Houston, Texas, are conducting clinical trials to determine whether ovarian cancer cells are sensitive to Gleevec.

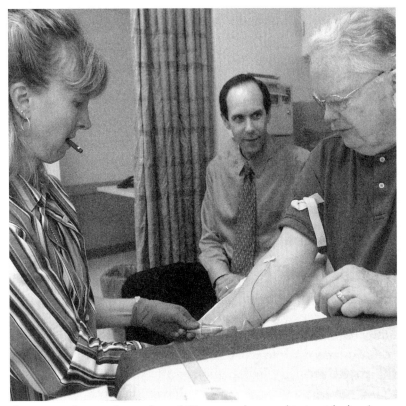

A cancer patient receives a dose of Gleevec, a drug used to treat leukemia. Researchers are studying the effectiveness of Gleevec in treating ovarian cancer.

Nell Alexander is a participant in the Houston trial. She has recurrent ovarian cancer that has proven to be resistant to standard chemotherapy. It is not yet known whether Gleevec will reduce or destroy Nell's tumor, but she is hopeful. "Gleevec was literally an answer to a prayer," she says. "Gleevec is my best chance because traditional chemotherapy is not going to work. If you give up and don't try, you are going to fail, so you don't give up and you try. Being in the trial has been worth it, even if it fails."[66]

Other scientists at Indiana University School of Medicine in Indianapolis are focusing on PCNA, a natural protein that inhibits cell division in mutated cells. These scientists theorize that in ovarian cancer, changes within mutated ovarian cancer cells limit, or even stop, the production of PCNA. This may be why mutated ovarian cancer cells divide and spread so rapidly. Therefore, these scientists are analyzing the molecular structure of healthy and malignant ovarian cells in order to determine if problems in PCNA protein production are, indeed, involved in the rapid spread of ovarian cancer. If such a connection is found, then work on a drug that stimulates PCNA production will begin.

Gene Therapy

Rather than using drugs to target mutant cells, other scientists are targeting genes as a treatment method. In a new process known as gene therapy, these scientists are attempting to replace mutant genes with normal genes. Scientists say that by controlling when

British scientists in the Imperial Cancer Research Fund in London are working on developing an anticancer gene that will help the body destroy malignant cells.

Spicy Food May Help Fight Cancer

Scientists are looking at the role certain foods play in cancer prevention and treatment. Among the foods being studied is capsaicin, which is the substance that makes chili peppers hot and is commonly used in Mexican cooking.

In 2003 a University of Texas at Austin study found that eating foods that contain capsaicin may destroy cancer cells. Scientists say that chemicals in capsaicin cause cancer cells to destroy themselves.

In an article in *Men's Health* magazine, Ruben Lotan, the director of the study, explains: "Capsaicin prevents structures within the cancerous cells from burning oxygen for energy. Without energy, the cells self-destruct."

Scientists do not know why capsaicin has this effect on cancer cells. More studies are planned. If capsaicin does prove to be as effective as the Texas study indicates, scientists will try to create a synthetic form of the spice that can be used in cancer treatment. In the meantime, in an effort to prevent cancer from developing, it cannot hurt healthy people to add more capsaicin to their diet.

Some scientists believe that people who eat lots of spicy Mexican food may benefit from the cancer-fighting properties of hot chili peppers.

ovarian cells divide and when cell division stops, the normal genes can stop the cancer process. Because existing cancer cells can no longer divide, they will die.

There have been a number of studies investigating the effectiveness of gene therapy in treating ovarian cancer. In fact, normal oncogenes and tumor suppressor genes, the genes that control cell division and growth, have already been grown in research laboratories. However, problems arise in getting the genes to ovarian cancer cells. Genes injected into the body cannot travel through the bloodstream on their own. They must be carried by something that can move easily through the bloodstream. And once in the bloodstream, there is no guarantee that the carrier will reach the cancerous cells.

Therefore, current research is focused on developing an effective gene delivery system. Scientists at the University of Alabama at Birmingham are hoping to use the common cold virus as a means of transport. Viruses can move freely through the bloodstream, and many viruses target specific organs. Moreover, once viruses reach their target they deliver their genes directly to a person's cells. In order to effectively use the cold virus, researchers are working on creating genetic modifications in the virus that would make it harmless. To do this, individual viruses are cultured and modified in a laboratory. Once this is done, scientists replace the genes with normal oncogenes or tumor suppressor genes. Other modifications cause the virus to target ovarian cancer cells. The virus is then injected into the patient's ovaries, where, scientists theorize, it will deposit the healthy genes and should reestablish normal cell growth.

Scientists have already made the necessary modifications in the virus, and hope to conduct clinical trials of the new delivery system in the near future. If the clinical trials prove successful, then gene therapy may become a safe and effective treatment for ovarian cancer, and may someday replace chemotherapy.

Other University of Alabama scientists are taking a similar approach, but instead of inserting normal genes into a modified cold virus that targets ovarian cancer cells, they are inserting the herpes virus gene. When the herpes virus gene is deposited inside an ovarian cancer cell, the cell appears to become susceptible to treatment with Ganciclovir, a herpes treatment drug. The medication attacks both the herpes virus, preventing it from infecting the patient, and the cancer cell it is lodged in. In 2002 Alabama scientists compared the effectiveness of this approach to the effectiveness of conventional chemotherapy using forty-one laboratory mice that had been injected with ovarian cancer cells. They found that the gene therapy mice had smaller tumors and lived longer than mice given chemotherapy treatment. In fact, after forty-five days of treatment, seven of the eleven mice in the gene therapy group were alive, while most of the other mice had died. After seventy-two days only two mice survived. Both had received gene therapy, and both showed no sign of ovarian cancer.

Based on these results, clinical trials have begun. Because this treatment targets and destroys only ovarian cancer cells, experts predict it will be easier for patients to tolerate than standard chemotherapy. Study director David T. Curiel explains: "In essence, we're giving local chemotherapy. Targeted directly to tumor cells, the new treatment spares healthy tissues, with many potential benefits."[67]

Other scientists are also using gene therapy to limit the damage chemotherapy inflicts on healthy cells. These scientists are working on injecting normal healthy cells with genes that block the destructive effects of chemotherapy, thereby making the treatment more effective. If this treatment proves successful, it would work like a locked door, keeping chemotherapy drugs from entering and destroying healthy cells. This would significantly lessen or eliminate most of the unpleasant side effects that chemotherapy causes. As a result, patients could be administered more frequent and higher doses of chemotherapy without risking damage to their health.

Antiangiogenesis

Another way gene therapy is being used is in a process known as antiangiogenesis. In order to grow, cancer cells must form a network of blood vessels, which supply the cells with blood, oxygen, and nutrients. The formation of this network is called angiogenesis. Antiangiogenesis shuts down this process.

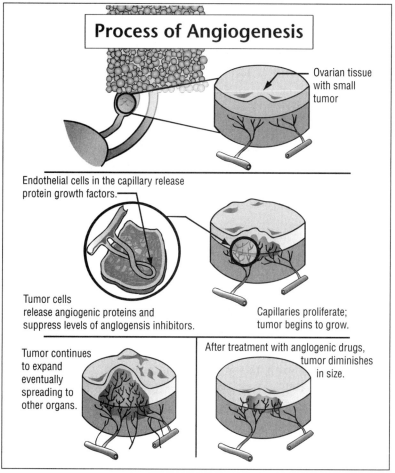

Process of Angiogenesis

Ovarian tissue with small tumor

Endothelial cells in the capillary release protein growth factors.

Tumor cells release angiogenic proteins and suppress levels of anglogensis inhibitors.

Capillaries proliferate; tumor begins to grow.

Tumor continues to expand eventually spreading to other organs.

After treatment with anglogenic drugs, tumor diminishes in size.

Scientists know that two genes, Id1 and Id3, help stimulate angiogenesis. Therefore, if these genes can be removed and replaced with modified genes that lack Id1 and Id3, scientists hypothesize that angiogenesis cannot occur.

National Cancer Institute scientists recently tested this theory on genetically engineered mice that lacked the two genes. The mice were injected with breast cancer cells. Although a breast cancer tumor did form at first, within a few weeks the tumor shrank and disappeared, and the mice showed no sign of cancer. All the mice in a control injected with the same cancer cells died.

When a similar test using lung cancer cells was administered, a tumor once again formed. This time the tumor did not shrink, but it did grow more slowly in the mutated mice than in the control group. No similar tests have been done on ovarian cancer cells. However, scientists say that depending on the type of cancer, removing Id1 and Id3 genes should slow down or prevent the growth and spread of cancer cells. Unfortunately, scientists have not yet developed a way to remove the genes in humans. Inserting genes is easier than removing them.

Researchers at the University of Chicago in 2002 inserted an antiangiogenesis gene called the tumor necrosis factor (TNF) directly into tumors of mice infected with cancer. TNF is an extremely powerful gene that cuts off the blood supply to both cancerous and healthy cells.

In this study, scientists modified the TNF gene so that it was activated by exposure to cisplatin, a chemotherapy drug used in treating ovarian cancer. Then, the mice were divided into four groups. The first group was treated with a combination of TNF and cisplatin. The next two groups were given only cisplatin or TNF. The control group received no treatment.

After two weeks, the tumors were compared. The control group's tumors grew to four times their original size. Those that were treated with either cisplatin or TNF alone also grew, but more slowly than those of the control group. Only the tumors of the group that were administered the combined therapy shrank significantly.

Scientists predict that this combination approach will someday be an effective treatment for ovarian cancer. However, because of the danger TNF poses to healthy cells, more research is necessary before the therapy can be used on humans.

Another approach to antiangiogenesis therapy, however, is much closer to widespread use. Scientists know that in order for angiogenesis to occur, cancer tumors send signals to surrounding tissue that stimulate the release of proteins needed to form new blood vessels. Scientists are testing a variety of different substances to stop those signals.

In fact, more than sixty different antiangiogenesis substances are being tested in clinical trials throughout the world. One such substance is the drug thalidomide. Administered to pregnant women for morning sickness in the 1950s, thalidomide hindered the development of limbs in fetuses whose mothers were administered the drug. Since blood vessels must form in order for a fetus to develop limbs, scientists theorize that in some manner thalidomide disrupts or blocks angiogenesis. Currently, this theory is being tested on women with ovarian cancer at M.D. Anderson Cancer Center, and the results are promising.

Harnessing the Immune System

Scientists at the University of California at Los Angeles are taking another approach to treating ovarian cancer. They are using antibodies, the substances the immune system produces to attack foreign invaders, to combat ovarian cancer cells. Normally, antibodies do not attack cancer cells because cancer cells arise from healthy cells and do not appear to be foreign to the body. However, cancer cells release certain chemicals and proteins that normal cells do not. For example, most ovarian cancer cells release CA-125.

Scientists have created a genetically modified antibody that recognizes CA-125 as an abnormal substance. They named the modified antibody OvaRex. When OvaRex is injected into the ovaries, it latches onto ovarian cancer cells that are secreting CA-125 and attacks the cells in the same way that antibodies normally attack foreign invaders.

Because the immune system is not always able to completely destroy foreign substances without the help of medication, scientists do not know if OvaRex alone is powerful enough to cure ovarian cancer. They do think that administering OvaRex after chemotherapy will destroy any cancer cells lingering in the body, and thus prolong a patient's remission period.

A 2003 clinical trial at UCLA tested OvaRex on 145 women with recurrent ovarian cancer. The women had completed their final chemotherapy cycle, and had responded well to the treatment. Once chemotherapy was complete, half the women were given injections of OvaRex, while half received a placebo. The placebo group relapsed in an average of eleven months, as opposed to twenty-four months for the OvaRex group.

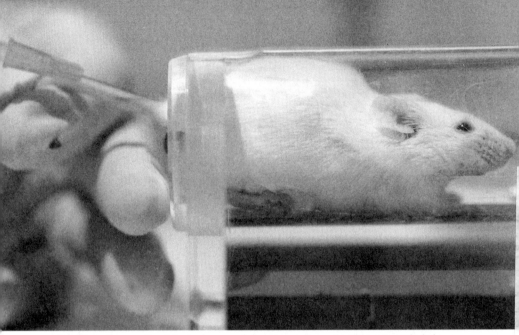

Based on the results of tests done on laboratory mice, scientists are optimistic that a vaccine to cure ovarian cancer can be developed in the near future.

The immune system also figures prominently in the development of a vaccine for ovarian cancer. As in OvaRex, scientists want to develop a vaccine for ovarian cancer patients that would provoke the immune system to attack ovarian cancer cells. In 2003 scientists at Norwegian Radium Hospital in Oslo developed a vaccine that provokes the immune system to attack cancer cells that produce a protein called telomerase. Telomerase is found in most cancer cells and is needed for cancer cells to divide.

The vaccine is currently being tested on eighty-five patients with pancreatic, lung, and skin cancer. Scientists are unsure whether the vaccine will work. So far, subjects with pancreatic cancer who received the highest dose of the vaccine have lived about a year longer than those who received a low dose. Therefore, researchers are hopeful.

As yet, the vaccine has not been tested on women with ovarian cancer, and its effectiveness in treating ovarian cancer still remains unclear. What is clear is that all the new treatments and diagnostic tests under development provide hope to women with ovarian cancer. "We really are on the cusp of a revolution in understanding this disease," explains ovarian cancer expert Michael Birrer of the National Cancer Institute. "I am optimistic."[68]

Notes

Introduction: When Knowledge Saves Lives

1. Quoted in Jera Stone, "Mother Exposes a 'Silent Killer,'" *Albuquerque Journal*, September 22, 2003, p. C2.
2. Sheryl Silver, "Ovarian Cancer: Symptoms Should Not Be Ignored," Women's Cancer Network, June 20, 2003. www.wcn.org/interior.cfm?featureid=2&contentfile=fa.cfm&contentid=10517&contenttypeid=8&featureid=2&diseaseid=13.
3. Quoted in Stone, "Mother Exposes a 'Silent Killer.'"
4. Quoted in Sheryl Silver, "Over 80,000 Women Newly Diagnosed Every Year," Women's Cancer Network, June 19, 2003. www.wcn.org/interior.cfm?featureid=2&contentfile=fa.cfm&contentid=10514&contenttype=8&featureid= 2&diseaseid=13.
5. George W. Bush, "National Ovarian Cancer Awareness Month: A Proclamation," The White House, September 1, 2003. www.whitehouse.gov/news/releases/2003/09/20030901-2.html.

Chapter 1: What Is Ovarian Cancer?

6. Quoted in Kristine Conner and Lauren Langford, *Ovarian Cancer: Your Guide to Taking Control*. Sebastopol, CA: O'Reilly, 2003, p. 14.
7. Gilda Radner, *It's Always Something*. New York: Simon & Schuster, 1989, pp. 83–84.
8. Radner, *It's Always Something*, p. 260.
9. Johns Hopkins Pathology: Ovarian Cancer, "Personal Stories: Cindy Melancon," www.ovariancancer.jhmi.edu/zstories2.cfm?personID=24&order=alpha.
10. Robin, interview with the author, June 17, 2004.

11. Liz Tilberis, *No Time to Die: Living with Ovarian Cancer*. Boston: Little, Brown, 1998, p. 33.
12. Robin, interview with the author.
13. Quoted in Conner and Langford, *Ovarian Cancer*, p. 42.
14. Quoted in Conner and Langford, *Ovarian Cancer*, p. 41.
15. Quoted in Conner and Langford, *Ovarian Cancer*, p. 44.
16. Quoted in Conner and Langford, *Ovarian Cancer*, p. 48.

Chapter 2: Confusing Symptoms and a Difficult Diagnosis

17. Johns Hopkins Pathology: Ovarian Cancer, "Personal Stories: Marian," www.ovariancancer.jhmi.edu/stories2.cf?personID=144&order=alpha.
18. Johns Hopkins Pathology: Ovarian Cancer, "Personal Stories: Cindy Melancon."
19. Anita, interview with the author, June 17, 2004.
20. Johns Hopkins Pathology: Ovarian Cancer, "Personal Stories: Charissa," www.ovariancancer.jhmi.edu/stories2.cf?personID=39&order=alpha.
21. Quoted in Conner and Langford, *Ovarian Cancer*, p. 63.
22. Johns Hopkins Pathology: Ovarian Cancer, "Personal Stories: Charissa."
23. Johns Hopkins Pathology: Ovarian Cancer, "Personal Stories: Christina Brown," www.ovariancancer.jhmi.edu/stories2.cfm?personID=7&order=alpha.
24. National Ovarian Cancer Coalition, "Surviving Ovarian Cancer: A Journey to Motherhood—Ramona—September, 2001." www.ovarian.org/pages.asp?page=surviving.
25. National Ovarian Cancer Coalition, "Surviving Ovarian Cancer: Betsy, Stage I." www.ovarian.org/pages.asp?page=surviving.
26. Quoted in Conner and Langford, *Ovarian Cancer*, p. 322.

Chapter 3: Conventional and Complementary Treatment

27. Quoted in Conner and Langford, *Ovarian Cancer*, p. 108.
28. Don S. Dizon, Nadeem R. Abu-Rustum, and Andrea Gibbs Brown, *100 Questions & Answers About Ovarian Cancer*. Boston: Jones and Bartlett, 2004, pp. 43–44.

29. National Ovarian Cancer Coalition, "Surviving Ovarian Cancer: A Journey to Motherhood—Ramona—September, 2001."
30. Quoted in Conner and Langford, *Ovarian Cancer*, p. 117.
31. Anita, interview with the author.
32. Radner, *It's Always Something*, p. 114.
33. Quoted in Conner and Langford, *Ovarian Cancer*, p. 181.
34. Quoted in Conner and Langford, *Ovarian Cancer*, p. 346.
35. Jimmie C. Holland and Sheldon Lewis, *The Human Side of Cancer: Living with Hope, Coping with Uncertainty*. New York: HarperCollins, 2000, p. 249.
36. Dizon, Abu-Rustum, and Brown, *100 Questions & Answers About Ovarian Cancer*, p. 75.
37. Radner, *It's Always Something*, p. 114.
38. Radner, *It's Always Something*, p. 114.
39. Anita, interview with the author.
40. Vivian Von Gruenigen, Bethan Powell, and Alice Spinelli, "Quality of Life," Gynecologic Cancer Foundation, www.thegcf.org/whatsnew/quality04.htm.
41. Quoted in Claudia Driefus, "A Hopeful Outlook on Taming Cancer," *AARP Bulletin*, December 2003, p. 13.
42. Dizon, Abu-Rustum, and Brown, *100 Questions & Answers About Ovarian Cancer*, p. 66.

Chapter 4: Living with Ovarian Cancer

43. Dizon, Abu-Rustum, and Brown, *100 Questions & Answers About Ovarian Cancer*, p. 107.
44. Quoted in Conner and Langford, *Ovarian Cancer*, pp. 182–83.
45. Dizon, Abu-Rustum, and Brown, *100 Questions & Answers About Ovarian Cancer*, p. 73.
46. Quoted in Conner and Langford, *Ovarian Cancer*, p. 423.
47. Dizon, Abu-Rustum, and Brown, *100 Questions & Answers About Ovarian Cancer*, p. 77.
48. Anita, interview with the author.
49. Anita, interview with the author.
50. Dizon, Abu-Rustum, and Brown, *100 Questions & Answers About Ovarian Cancer*, p. 106.
51. Radner, *It's Always Something*, p. 116.

52. Radner, *It's Always Something*, p. 116.
53. Quoted in Look Good . . . Feel Better, "Kathleen J. Nelson," www.lookgoodfeelbetter.org/audience/press/press_re leases/kathleen_nelson.htm.
54. Quoted in Conner and Langford, *Ovarian Cancer*, p. 360.
55. Quoted in Conner and Langford, *Ovarian Cancer*, p. 366.
56. Quoted in Holland and Lewis, *The Human Side of Cancer*, p. 140.
57. Quoted in Conner and Langford, *Ovarian Cancer*, pp. 156–57.
58. Quoted in Conner and Langford, *Ovarian Cancer*, p. 158.
59. Quoted in Radner, *It's Always Something*, p. 142.
60. Radner, *It's Always Something*, p. 267.

Chapter 5: What the Future Holds

61. Quoted in National Cancer Institute, "Protein Patterns May Identify Ovarian Cancer," February 7, 2002. www.nci.nih.gov /newscenter/proteomics07feb02.
62. Quoted in Judy Foreman, "On the Verge of an Ovarian Cancer Test," National Ovarian Cancer Coalition, May 4, 2004. www.ovarian.org/press.asp?releaseID=269.
63. Quoted in Susan Gaidos, "View to a Cell," *Dallas Morning News*, December 9, 2002, p. 1C.
64. Quoted in Susan Gaidos, "View to a Cell," p. 6C
65. Wendy Elliman, "From Radiology to Radiance," *Hadassah*, May 2003, p. 60.
66. Quoted in CancerWise, "Gleevec Offers Hope to Ovarian Cancer Patients," September 2002. www.cancerwise.org/ september_2002/index.cfm.
67. Quoted in UAB Health System, "UAB-Pioneered Ovarian Cancer Gene Therapy," www.health.uab.edu/show.asp? durki=51529.
68. Michael Birrer, "Molecular Biology of Ovarian Cancer with Emphasis on Molecular Targets," Gynecologic Cancer Foundation, www.thegcf.org/whatsnew/molecular04.htm.

Glossary

abdominal cavity: The part of the body that is bordered by the lungs and diaphragm on top, and by the pubic bone on the bottom.

angiogenesis: The growth and formation of blood vessels, which provide healthy and cancerous cells with oxygen and nutrients carried in the blood.

antiangiogenesis: A process that blocks the formation of blood vessels, which provide cancer cells with blood needed for their growth.

antibodies: Chemicals produced by the immune system that attack and destroy harmful substances.

antioxidants: Vitamins that contain chemicals that prevent oxygen molecules in the body from damaging cells.

ascites: Waste fluid that often builds up in the stomachs of women with ovarian cancer.

benign tumor: An abnormal growth composed of harmless noncancerous cells.

BRCA1 and BRCA2: Tumor suppressor genes, which may be mutated in people with ovarian cancer.

CA-125: A protein found in ovarian cancer cells.

cyst: An abnormal growth that is filled with fluid.

debulking: The surgical removal of cancer cells from the body.

gene therapy: A form of treatment that replaces mutated genes with healthy ones.

gynecologist: A doctor who specializes in treating the female reproductive system.

gynecologic cancer: Any cancer of a woman's reproductive organs.

gynecologic oncologist: A doctor who treats cancer of the female reproductive system.

laparoscope: A lighted flexible tubular instrument with a cameralike device on the tip.

laparotomy: Surgery to diagnose ovarian cancer.

malignant tumor: An abnormal growth composed of cancer cells.

metastasis: The process in which cancer cells spread from one part of the body to another.

molecular imaging: A form of imaging that produces images of targeted cells and the molecules that make up the cells.

oncogene: A gene that signals cells to divide.

oncologist: A doctor who specializes in treating cancer patients.

oophorectomy: An operation in which the ovaries are removed.

ovaries: Two small oval organs that are part of a woman's reproductive system. The ovaries produce eggs at monthly intervals that are either fertilized or shed from the body when a woman menstruates.

ovulation: The monthly process in which eggs are released from the ovaries.

Pap test: A test in which cells taken from inside a woman's vagina are examined for evidence of cervical cancer.

protease: A chemical that breaks downs connective tissues, allowing cancer cells to enter different organs.

proteomics: The study of proteins in cells, tissues, and blood.

radical hysterectomy: An operation in which the ovaries, fallopian tubes, uterus, and cervix are removed.

shedding: The process in which cancer cells break free from a tumor.

spectroscope: A machine that uses heat waves to produce images of protein patterns in the bloodstream.

tumor: An abnormal mass or growth.

tumor suppressor gene: A gene that signals cells to stop dividing.

Organizations to Contact

American Cancer Society
1599 Clifton Rd. NE
Atlanta, GA 30329
(800) 227-2345
www.cancer.org
The American Cancer Society is a national organization with local groups throughout the country. It offers information on all types of cancer and sponsors support groups throughout the United States.

Gilda Radner Familial Ovarian Cancer Registry
Roswell Park Cancer Institute
Elm and Carlton Streets
Buffalo, NY 14263
(800) 682-7426
www.ovariancancer.com
An international registry for people with two or more relatives with ovarian cancer. The organization uses the information for ovarian cancer research. It also offers telephone help, genetic counseling, and information.

Gilda's Club
322 Eighth Ave., Suite 1402
New York, NY 10001
(888) 445-3248
E-mail info@gildasclub.org
www.gildasclub.org
With locations throughout the country, Gilda's Club offers information, programs, and support for people with all types of cancer, and for their loved ones.

International Ovarian Cancer Connection
PO Box 7948
Amarillo, TX 79114
(806) 355-2565
E-mail chmelancon@aol.com
www.ovarian-news.org
The International Ovarian Cancer Connection provides support for ovarian cancer patients by matching them with ovarian cancer survivors. Publishes *Conversations!*, a monthly newsletter about ovarian cancer.

National Ovarian Cancer Coalition
2335 E. Atlantic Blvd., Suite 401
Pompano Beach, FL 33062
(888) 682-7426
E-mail NOCC@ovarian.org
www.ovarian.org
Founded by ovarian cancer survivors, the coalition promotes ovarian cancer awareness. It provides information and news on ovarian cancer.

Ovarian Cancer National Alliance
1627 K St. NW, 12th Floor
Washington, DC 20006
(202) 331-1332
E-mail ovarian@aol.com
www.ovariancancer.org
Dedicated to educating the public about ovarian cancer. This organization lobbies for ovarian cancer research and hosts ovarian cancer meetings and conferences.

The Wellness Community
35 E. Seventh St., Suite 412
Cincinnati, OH 45202
(888) 793-9355
E-mail help@thewellnesscommunity.org
www.thewellnesscommunity.org
A national organization that offers support and educational workshops for cancer patients and their loved ones in comfortable settings throughout the United States.

For Further Reading

Books

American Cancer Society, *American Cancer Society's Guide to Complementary and Alternative Cancer Methods*. Atlanta, GA: American Cancer Society, 2000. An extensive look at different alternative and complementary methods used in treating cancer.

Ellen Dorfman and Heidi Schultz Adams, *Here and Now: Inspiring Stories of Cancer Survivors*. New York: Marlowe, 2002. Thirty-eight cancer survivors tell their stories.

Kirsten Lamb, *Cancer*. Austin, TX: Raintree Steck-Vaughn, 2003. A simple book on cancer covering diagnosis, treatment, and prevention.

Lisa Yount, *Cancer*. San Diego, CA: Greenhaven Press, 2000. Talks about the cause, effects, prevention, detection, and treatment of cancer.

Web Sites

CancerWise (www.cancerwise.org). Sponsored by the M.D. Anderson Cancer Center, this Web site provides news and information on every type of cancer.

Gynecologic Cancer Foundation (www.thegcf.org). Offers information, free publications, and research news on all types of gynecologic cancers. Links to the Women's Cancer Network.

Johns Hopkins Pathology: Ovarian Cancer Web (www.ovarian cancer.jhmi.edu). Johns Hopkins Cancer Center offers information about ovarian cancer, including treatment options and support. Ovarian cancer survivors offer their point of view.

Look Good . . . Feel Better (www.lookgoodfeelbetter.org). Provides information on living with cancer and adjusting to the physical changes the disease causes.

Memorial Sloan-Kettering Cancer Center (www.mskcc.org). Offers a wealth of material about all types of cancer, with a section devoted to ovarian cancer.

National Cancer Institute (www.nci.nih.gov). Provides information and free booklets on every type of cancer. Lists clinical trials and discusses current research.

Planet Cancer (www.planetcancer.org). An organization that helps young people with cancer support each other.

Women's Cancer Network (www.wcn.org). Sponsors ovarian cancer public awareness activities, along with offering information about ovarian and other gynecologic cancers.

Works Consulted

Books

Kristine Conner and Lauren Langford, *Ovarian Cancer: Your Guide to Taking Control*. Sebastopol, CA: O'Reilly, 2003. A comprehensive resource book dealing with all aspects of ovarian cancer.

Don S. Dizon, Nadeem R. Abu-Rustum, and Andrea Gibbs Brown, *100 Questions & Answers About Ovarian Cancer*. Boston: Jones and Bartlett, 2004. Using questions and answers, this book gives information about ovarian cancer from a doctor's and a patient's point of view.

Jimmie C. Holland and Sheldon Lewis, *The Human Side of Cancer: Living with Hope, Coping with Uncertainty*. New York: Harper-Collins, 2000. Deals with the emotional issues people with cancer face from diagnosis to living with cancer.

Gilda Radner, *It's Always Something*. New York: Simon & Schuster, 1989. The comedian tells about her fight against ovarian cancer in a humorous manner.

Liz Tilberis, *No Time to Die: Living with Ovarian Cancer*. Boston: Little, Brown, 1998. An ovarian cancer patient describes her life with ovarian cancer.

Periodicals

Associated Press, "Pumping Iron Seen as Having Benefit in Cancer Fight," *Las Cruces Sun News*, October 14, 2003.

Claudia Dreifus, "A Hopeful Outlook on Taming Cancer," *AARP Bulletin*, December 2003.

Wendy Elliman, "From Radiology to Radiance," *Hadassah*, May 2003.

Susan Gaidos, "View to a Cell," *Dallas Morning News*, December 9, 2002.

Gilda Radner Ovarian Cancer Registry Newsletter, "Hormone Replacement Therapy: Risk of Breast or Ovarian Cancer," Spring 2004.

Francesca Lunzer Kritz, "Ovarian Cancer Awareness Bill," *Jewish Weekly*, May 14, 2004.

Las Cruces Sun News, "Web Site Offers Information on Alternative Medicines," June 18, 2004.

Men's Health, "Nutrition Bulletin," January/February 2003.

Jera Stone, "Mother Exposes a 'Silent Killer,'" *Albuquerque Journal*, September 22, 2003.

Lindsey Tanner, "3 Symptoms Raise Alert," *Albuquerque Journal*, June 9, 2004.

Internet Sources

Michael Birrer, "Molecular Biology of Ovarian Cancer with Emphasis on Molecular Targets," Gynecologic Cancer Foundation, www.thegcf.org/whatsnew/molecular04.htm.

George W. Bush, "National Ovarian Cancer Awareness Month: A Proclamation," The White House, September 1, 2003. www.whitehouse.gov/news/releases/2003/09/20030901-2.html.

CancerWise, "Gleevec Offers Hope to Ovarian Cancer Patients," September 2002. www.cancerwise.org/september_2002/index.cfm.

Judy Foreman, "On the Verge of an Ovarian Cancer Test," National Ovarian Cancer Coalition, May 4, 2004. www.ovarian.org/press.asp?releaseID=269.

Christine Gorman and Alice Parker, "The Fires Within," Time.com, February 23, 2004. www.time.com/time/magazine/article/subscriber/0,10987,1101040223-590682,00.html.

Johns Hopkins Pathology: Ovarian Cancer, "Personal Stories: Charissa," www.ovariancancer.jhmi.edu/stories2.cfm?personID=39&order=alpha.

————, "Personal Stories: Christina Brown," www.ovarian-cancer.jhmi.edu/stories2.cfm?personID=7&order=alpha.

————, "Personal Stories: Cindy Melancon," www. ovariancancer. jhmi.edu/stories2.cfm?personID=24&order=alpha.

————, "Personal Stories: Marian," www.ovariancancer.jhmi .edu /stories2.cfm?personID=144&order=alpha.

Look Good . . . Feel Better, "Kathleen S. Nelson," www.lookgood feelbetter.org/audience/press/press_releases/kathleen_ nelson.htm.

National Cancer Institute, "Protein Patterns May Identify Ovar-ian Cancer," February 7, 2002. www.nci.nih.gov/newscenter /proteomics07feb02.

National Ovarian Cancer Coalition, "Surviving Ovarian Cancer: A Journey to Motherhood—Ramona—September, 2001." www. ovarian.org/pages.asp?page=surviving.

————, "Surviving Ovarian Cancer: Betsy, Stage I," www.ovarian. org/pages.asp?page=surviving.

Sheryl Silver, "Ovarian Cancer: Symptoms Should Not Be Ig-nored," Women's Cancer Network, June 20, 2003. www.wcn. org/interior.cfm?featureid=2&contentfile=fa.cfm&content id=10517&contenttypeid=8&featureid=2&diseaseid=13.

————, "Over 80,000 Women Newly Diagnosed Every Year," Women's Cancer Network, June 19, 2003. www.wcn.org/inte rior.cfm?featureid=2&contentfile=fa.cfm&contentid=10514& contenttypeid=8&featureid=2&diseaseid=13.

UAB Health System, "UAB-Pioneered Ovarian Cancer Gene Therapy," www.health.uab.edu/show.asp?durki=51529.

Vivian Von Gruenigen, Bethan Powell, and Alice Spinelli, "Qual-ity of Life," Gynecologic Cancer Foundation, www.thegcf.org /whatsnew/quality04.htm.

Index

AARP Bulletin (Dreifus), 80
abdomen
  cell diagnostics and, 42
  debulking and, 48
  exploratory surgery and, 38
  imaging tests and, 72
  ovarian Pap test and, 81
  pain and, 18, 30
  pelvic exam and, 34
  peritoneum and, 17
  radiation treatment and, 55
  swelling of, 8, 20, 32
Abu-Rustum, Nadeem R., 16
Albuquerque Journal (newspaper), 32
Alexander, Nell, 84
American Cancer Online Resources
  (ACOR), 77
American Cancer Society, 32, 59, 70
angiogenesis, 88–91
antiangiogenesis, 88, 90–91
antibodies, 15, 91
antioxidants, 60–61
appetite, loss of, 66
ascites, 20
Aykroyd, Dan, 24

Belushi, John, 24
Benjamin, Harold, 77
Birrer, Michael, 92
birth control. *See* contraceptives
bladder, 16–18, 33, 42, 48
blood cells, red, 51, 58, 63–64
blood cells, white, 15, 17, 51, 58
brain, 15, 18, 42
BRCA1 and BRCA2, 22–23, 26, 28
breast cancer
  Id1 and Id3 and, 89
  ovarian cancer risks and, 20, 23
  prevalence of, 8
  protein patterns and, 79

screening, 11
Brown, Andrea Gibbs
  on activities, 69
  on antinausea medication, 56, 65
  on appetite loss, 66
  on fatigue, 62
  on fertility loss, 48
  on meditation, 60
  on ovarian function, 16
Bush, George W., 12

Cancer Care, 70
Candy, John, 24
CA-125, 36–37, 51–52, 72, 91
capsaicin, 86
carboplatin, 50
CAT scan, 37
Cedars-Sinai Medical Center, 81
cells
  DNA and, 51
  epithelial, 40–41, 44, 50, 78, 82
  germ, 40–41
  microtubules and, 51
  PCNA and, 84–85
  sex cord-stromal, 40–41, 50
  shedding, 17–18
  telomerase and, 92
Center for Biologics Evaluation and
  Research, 78
cervix, 16, 18, 28, 81
chemotherapy
  advanced cancer and, 50
  cisplatin and, 90
  complementary and alternative
    treatments and, 46, 58, 60–61
  cycles of, 52, 82
  emotional issues and, 72–73
  fatigue and, 62–63
  gene therapy and, 87–88
  hair loss and, 70–71

infections and, 64–65
loss of appetite/weight loss and, 66–67, 69
monitoring after completion of, 70
nausea and, 65–66
OvaRex and, 91
pain and, 69–70
port-a-catheter and, 51, 53
recurrence of cancer and, 55
remission and, 52–53
resistant cells and, 82–84
side effects of, 56–58
steroids and, 51
as surgical alternative, 49
visualization and, 59
cisplatin, 90
clinical trials, 53
antiangiogenesis substances and, 90
experimental drugs and, 55
Gleevec and, 83
ovarian Pap test and, 82
viral delivery systems and, 87–88
see also research
colon, 8, 17–18
complementary/alternative medicine (CAM), 58
computerized axial tomography. See CAT scan
Conner, Kristine, 26
constipation
antinausea medication and, 56, 65
cancer symptoms and, 18, 30–31, 33
hydration and, 65
nutrition and, 61
contraceptives, 26–27
Curiel, David T., 88

debulking, 46, 48–50
dehydration, 65
detection, 11–12, 34–35, 78–79, 82
diagnosis, 30–31, 38, 45
diaphragm, 18, 38, 42, 48
diet. *See* nutrition
digestion, 19, 30–31, 43, 56, 61
Dizon, Don, 16
Dreifus, Claudia, 80
drugs
antinausea, 65
combination, 46, 52, 55
experimental, 55
fertility, 26–27
Ganciclovir, 88

hormone replacement therapy and, 26, 28
mitotic inhibitors, 51
molecular imaging and, 82
steroids, 51, 56
target, 83–85
thalidomide, 90–91
see also medications

eggs, 13, 16, 21, 41
emotional issues, 62, 72–73, 76
endorphins, 69
epithelial ovarian cancer, 40–41, 44, 50, 78, 82
estrogen, 13, 16, 28, 62
ethnic links, 23
exercise, 67–69

fallopian tubes, 16–18, 21, 28, 46
fatigue
as cancer symptom, 8, 30
chemotherapy and, 51, 56, 58–59
coping with, 62–64
exercise and, 68–69
hydration and, 65
feces, 18, 65
fertility, 13, 16, 21–22, 46, 48
Food and Drug Administration (FDA), 58, 78
Fox Chase Cancer Center, 83

Ganciclovir, 88
gene(s)
antiangiogenesis and, 88–91
BRCA, 23
cell mutation and, 13, 15
Id1 and Id3, 89–90
suppressor, 13, 15, 22, 87
therapy, 85, 87–88
TNF, 90
treatment and, 80, 85
gene therapy, 85, 87–88
Gilda Radner Familial Ovarian Cancer Registry, 28
Gilda's Club, 25, 76–77
Gleevec, 83–84
Godspell (musical), 24
Goff, Barbara, 8, 32
Gordon, Johanna Silver, 43
Gordon, Sheryl Silver, 43
Gostout, Bobbie, 11
Gynecological Cancer Education and Awareness Act, 43
gynecologic cancer, 11, 43

Gynecologic Cancer Foundation, 11, 58
gynecologist, 34

Hadassah Hospital, 83
hair loss, 51, 56–57, 70–71
Haunted Honeymoon (movie), 24
heredity, 22, 26
Holland, Jimmie C., 55, 73
hormone replacement therapy, 26, 28
Human Side of Cancer, The (Holland and Lewis), 73
hydration, 65
hysterectomy, 28, 46, 48–49

Id1 and Id3, 89–90
Indiana University School of Medicine, 84
infection
avoiding, 64–65
blood cells and, 51, 58
surgery and, 49
urinary tract, 31, 33
intercourse, 30
intestines, 18–19, 33, 42, 48
intravenous feeding, 46, 50–52
It's Always Something (Radner), 24, 75

Jewish Week (newspaper), 43
Johanna's Law, 43
Johns Hopkins University, 49

Karlan, Beth Y., 81
kidneys, 18–19, 48, 55
Kotz, Herbert, 33
Kritz, Francesca Lunzer, 43

Langford, Lauren, 26
laparoscope, 81–82
laparotomy, 38
Larrison, Evelyn, 65
Las Cruces Sun News (newspaper), 68
Levin, Sander, 43
Lewis, Sheldon, 55, 73
Lichtman, Jeff, 82
Look Good…Feel Better (organization), 70–71
Lotan, Ruben, 86
lung cancer, 8, 18, 42, 89, 92
lymphatic system, 17, 20
lymph nodes, 38, 42, 48

Massachusetts Institute of

Technology, 15
M.D. Anderson Cancer Center, 60, 83, 91
medications
chemotherapy and, 46, 50, 65–66, 82, 88
clinical trials and, 53
emotional issues and, 73
erythropoietin and, 63–64
intravenous, 51
for pain, 69
resistance to, 55
see also drugs
meditation, 60
Melancon, Cindy, 20, 33
melatonin, 62
menopause, 16, 21–22, 28, 30
menstruation, 13, 16, 20–22, 36, 41
metastasis, 17–18, 26, 34, 36, 41–42
microtubules, 51
mitotic inhibitors, 51
molecular imaging, 82–83
mutation, 13, 15, 23, 26–28

National Cancer Institute
alternative treatment and, 59
angiogenesis and, 89
blood test development, 78
Breast and Gynecologic Cancer Research Group and, 27
goals of, 80
proteomics tests and, 81
National Ovarian Cancer Association, 69
National Ovarian Cancer Coalition, 22
National Ovarian Cancer Early Detection Program and Genetic Study, 82
nausea/vomiting, 56, 59, 65–66
Northwestern University, 81–82
Norwegian Radium Hospital, 92
nutrition, 60–61, 66–67, 75, 86

oncogene, 13, 15, 87
oncologists, 33, 49
100 Questions and Answers About Ovarian Cancer (Dizon, Abu-Rustum, and Brown), 16
oophorectomy, 28–29
oral contraceptives, 26–27
OvaRex, 91–92
Ovarian Cancer Awareness Month, 12

Ovarian Cancer National Alliance, 22
ovarian Pap tests, 81–82
Ovarian Problems Discussion List,
77
ovaries
cancer stage/grade and, 42
eptithelial cells and, 40
estrogen production and, 62
examinations of, 34
exploratory surgery of, 34, 38
function of, 13, 16
hysterectomy and, 28–29, 46, 48
OvaRex and, 91
ovarian Pap test and, 81–82
puberty and, 20–21
sex cord-stromal cells and, 41
transvaginal ultrasound and, 37
virus delivery system and, 87
see also cells
ovulation, 16, 22, 28

pain
cancer symptoms and, 18–19,
30–31
chemotherapy and, 56
coping with, 69
during intercourse, 30
pancreatic cancer, 92
Pap test, 81–82
pathologists, 38, 40–42
PCNA, 84–85
pelvis
cancer cells and, 18
cancer stages and, 38
exploratory surgery and, 38, 42
imaging tests and, 72
ovaries, location in, 13, 16, 34
symptomatic pain and, 30
Peretz, Tamar, 83
peritoneum, 17–18
Piwnica-Worms, David, 83
Place of Wellness, 60
port-a-catheter, 51, 53
progesterone, 16
prognosis, 44–45, 48–49, 78
prostate cancer, 23
protease, 17
protein patterns, 79
proteomics, 78, 81, 83
puberty, 20–21

radiation, 55, 79, 81
Radner, Gilda, 24–25
family cancer history of, 23

Gilda Radner Familial Ovarian
Cancer Registry, 28
Gilda's Club and, 25
on hair loss, 57, 70
Saturday Night Live and, 24
on sense of taste, 56
on spread of cancer, 18–19
on steroids, 51
on support, 77
on visualization, 59
Wellness Community and, 75
rectum, 16, 34, 48
recurrence, 46, 52–53, 55, 62, 72–73,
91
remission, 46, 52–53, 55, 78, 91
research
alternative treatment and, 58
diagnostic testing and, 78, 81
exercise and, 69
gene therapy and, 87
immune system vaccines and, 92–93
nutrition and, 66
oral contraceptives and, 27–28
sleep and, 62
spicy foods and, 86
TNF and, 90
treatment and, 78, 80
see also clinical trials
risk factor(s)
age as, 20–21, 24, 31, 41, 44
awareness of, 11–12
genetics and, 22–23, 26
ovulation and, 22
preventive measures, 26–29, 69
Rodriguez, Carmen, 32

Saturday Night Live (TV show), 24
screening, 11, 26, 36, 81
Second City Improvisional Troupe,
24
sex cord-stromal cells, 40–41, 50
skin cancer, 92
spectroscope, 79, 81
spleen, 48
Stanford University School of
Medicine, 62
steroids, 51, 56
stomach, 18, 20, 42, 83
studies. *See* research
support
centers/programs, 25
family, 12
group, 74, 76–77
Look Good…Feel Better, 70

psychiatrists, 73
Wellness Community, 75
surgery
    alternative treatments and, 58–59,
        61
    diagnostic, 30, 32, 38
    exploratory, 34, 38, 42
    fertility-sparing, 46, 48
    ovarian Pap test and, 81
    pain and, 69
    preventive, 26, 28–29
    risks of, 49
surveys/statistics
    on diagnosis, 8, 32
    on hair loss, 70–71
    on prognosis, 44
survival rate, 11, 42, 44–45, 52, 79,
    81
symptoms, 8–11, 30–34, 45
see also specific symptoms

Tanner, Lindsey, 32
    telomerase, 92
    tests, diagnostic
    biopsies and, 38, 42, 46
    blood, 78–79, 81
    imaging, 37–38, 72
    medical exams and, 26
    pelvic exams, 34–35
    proteomics and, 81
    stage/grade determination and,
        41–42
    X-rays, 72
    see also research
thalidomide, 90–91
Tilberis, Liz, 21
transvaginal ultrasound, 37
treatment
    CAM and, 58
    clinical trials and, 53
    complementary, 58–60
    debulking and, 46, 48–49
    diet and, 60–61
    early diagnosis and, 11–12
    exploratory surgery and, 38
    gene therapy, 87–88
    OvaRex and, 91–92
    radiation and, 55
    side effects of, 56–58

spicy foods and, 86
tumor growth and, 41
see also chemotherapy;
    medications; research
Trimble, Edward, 49
tumor necrosis factor (TNF), 90
tumors, 15
    benign, 15, 35–36, 38–39
    CAT scans and, 37–38
    cysts and, 35, 38
    estrogen and, 28
    malignant, 15, 28, 38, 40–41, 85
    organ obstruction and, 18–20
    pelvic, 32, 34
    protein patterns of, 79
    recurrent, 55
    spread of, 17–18, 53
    weak points of, 83
    see also cells; gene(s); treatment
tyrosine kinases, 83

ultrasound, 26, 37–38
University of Alabama at
    Birmingham, 87–88
University of California at Los
    Angeles (UCLA), 91
University of Chicago, 81, 90
urine, 19
uterus
    cancer cells and, 42
    hysterectomy and, 46, 48
    reproductive system and, 16, 22
    tumors and, 17–18

vagina, 16, 30, 34, 37, 42
Van Seiden, Michael, 73
von Eschenbach, Andrew C., 59, 80
Von Gruenigen, Vivian, 58
vulva, 16

Washington University's Molecular
    Imaging Center, 82
Weinberg, Robert A., 58
Wellness Community, 75, 77
Wilder, Gene, 24
Woman in Red, The, (movie), 24

Zoon, Kathryn, 78

Picture Credits

Cover photo: © Custom Medical Stock Photo

About the Author

Barbara Sheen has been an author and educator for more than thirty years. Her fiction and nonfiction have been published in the United States and Europe. She writes in English and Spanish. She lives in New Mexico with her family. In her spare time, she enjoys swimming, gardening, bicycling, cooking, and reading.